KIDNAPPED

BOOK ONE:
THE ABDUCTION

GORDON KORMAN
TAKES YOU TO THE EDGE OF ADVENTURE

WWW.SCHOLASTIC.COM
WWW.GORDONKORMAN.COM

GORDON KORMAN

KIDNAPPED

BOOK ONE

THE
ABDUCTION

SCHOLASTIC INC.

New York   Toronto   London   Auckland   Sydney
Mexico City   New Delhi   Hong Kong   Buenos Aires

ISBN-13: 978-0-439-84777-3
ISBN-10: 0-439-84777-X

24 23 22 21 20 19 18 17 16 15   12 13 14 15 16/0

Printed in the U.S.A.   40

First printing, May 2006

For Jay

PROLOGUE

INNOCENT!!!

AMALGAMATED PRESS

BALTIMORE, MD.

Doctors John and Louise Falconer are home again. Fourteen months into life sentences for aiding foreign terrorists, shocking new evidence proved they had been framed. HORUS Global Group, a front for the terrorists, has been found responsible. All HORUS agents are believed to be either dead or behind bars at this time.

The Falconers are joined by their children, Aiden, 15, and Margaret, 11, who achieved almost as much notoriety as their parents in recent months. The two escaped from juvenile detention in Nebraska and became fugitives for eight weeks, logging more than 7,000 miles as they eluded the FBI, the juvenile authorities, and dozens of state and local police forces. All charges against them were dropped upon their parents' release.

The family declined an interview, stating only that they intended to put the episode behind them. "We've

had enough of headlines," Dr. John Falconer told re-
porters. "What we want—what we pray for—is just
to get back to normal."

1

Normal.

Meg couldn't hold back a bitter laugh. Like anything would ever be normal again, after Mom and Dad had been locked up for more than a year, and she and Aiden had been hunted like animals by the police, not to mention a professional killer. After their pictures had been displayed in newspapers and on TV. After the name "Falconer" had been turned into a synonym for *traitor*.

She surveyed the bustling playground. *This* was normal. Lunch recess — seventh grade. A babble of animated voices, hundreds of middle schoolers playing sports, running, wrestling, shouting . . .

And me in the middle of it, reflected Meg, *trying to pretend that I care about a pickup baseball game when I've lived through things other kids couldn't imagine in their wildest nightmares.*

"Strike one!"

Lost in her thoughts, Meg didn't even see the first pitch sail by. There were snickers around the diamond.

It was hard to believe that this group had once been her friends. They had shared classes and summer camps, birthday parties and sleepovers. Now they seemed so clueless, so innocent. Like kindergartners, almost . . .

"Strike two!"

She stepped out of the batter's box as the catcher threw back the ball.

"Hey!" stage-whispered Wendell Butz from third base. "Let's watch the traitor strike out!"

White-hot anger exploded inside her chest. Bad enough that Mom and Dad had suffered so much in prison. Bad enough that their children had been turned into outlaws . . .

But it's supposed to be OVER!

It was a rage too powerful for Meg to control. She drew back the bat and let fly. Spinning like a boomerang, the aluminum projectile missed Wendell's head and spiraled into foul territory. It smacked into the flagpole, knocking off the rusted metal cleat. The flag plunged forty feet to land in a heap in the grass.

There were three sharp blasts on a whistle.

The principal's office. Once upon a time, she'd been afraid of it. That fear seemed ridiculous now. How could a pudgy middle-aged guy intimidate her after she'd faced a killer?

Dr. Barstow did not look friendly. "I hope you have an explanation for what happened today, Meg."

She studied the carpet. "I lost my cool." What would be the point of ratting out Wendell, even though the jerk deserved it?

"The flag is the symbol of our country," the principal said sternly. "It must never be allowed to touch the ground."

Wait a minute—I nearly took Wendell's head off, and all Dr. Barstow cares about is the flag?

"That wasn't on purpose!" Meg defended herself. "If I could hit a doohickey on the side of a pole with a baseball bat from twenty yards away, I wouldn't be here; I'd be at the Olympic trials."

"That'll do," the principal admonished. "I'd think that somebody from *your* family would take special care to be respectful of the flag."

"My parents are innocent!" Meg stormed. "And even after everything that's happened, they still love their country. If that's not patriotism, what is?"

One glance at Dr. Barstow's cold granite expression, and Meg just knew. There were Falconer haters out there—people who would never accept that Mom and Dad had been cleared. And Meg's own principal was one of them.

Will we ever get our lives back?

With great concentration, Aiden Falconer formed the coarse yarn into three rings and began to loop the free end through them. At that moment, the bus hit a bump, and the plant hanger he'd been working on converted itself to a tangle of twine in his lap.

Macramé, he thought in disgust. It was impossible to do macramé in a moving vehicle. The only reason he was in this stupid class was because he'd started school late. Macramé had been the only elective still open.

Last year, his elective had been Enriched Science Independent Study. He and Richie Pembleton had been building a Foucault pendulum for the science fair. It had only been half finished when the Falconer family nightmare had whisked him away. Even working alone, Richie had managed to place third at district. If Aiden had been there, Richie was sure they would have won.

Aiden craned his neck to look at his onetime best friend a few rows back, hidden beneath the Greenville Cubs baseball cap the boy never took off. It was not the science fair that bothered Richie. It was the Aiden Falconer who had returned from his ordeal — experienced, hardened, bitter. Aiden found it impossible to slip back into the regular comfortable ways with his buddy. The chess club held no interest for someone who had once gambled on strategies with his own life and that of his sister hanging in the balance. The old shared jokes weren't funny anymore.

Nothing's funny anymore.

Richie was still Richie, but Aiden was forever changed.

It was one more thing his family's disaster had cost him. Not the biggest, certainly. But it was still sad.

The bus swung into the driveway of the middle school and lurched to a halt. He watched the newcomers filing aboard.

"Hey, bro." Meg took the empty seat beside him. She indicated the spaghetti of limp yarn in his lap. "Hang yourself yet?"

"If I hang myself with macramé," he assured her darkly, "it won't be by accident." He noticed the redness of her eyes behind the joking smile. "What?"

Barely concealing her anger, Meg told him about the incident at recess. "The minute that flag hit the ground, Barstow acted like I did it because all Falconers must be terrorists."

"Take it easy," Aiden soothed. "People get crazy about flags. There are complicated rules about how to fold them and handle them. If they touch the ground, that's a definite no-no."

She was bitter. "How was I supposed to know that cleat was rusted through?"

"It's not your fault the guy's sensitive."

"He's not sensitive — he hates us," she shot back. "Why can't people accept that Mom and Dad are innocent, and our family isn't the enemy anymore?"

Nowhere was that question more resounding than inside the Falconer home. The CRIME SCENE tape had been removed. There was a new front door replacing the one that had been bashed into toothpicks by an FBI battering ram. John and Louise Falconer had been reinstated as professors at the college. But they were on "research leave." Which really meant that nobody wanted to study criminology with professors who had once been called the worst traitors in half a century.

In the meantime, Mom was throwing herself into the task of getting the house back in shape. Dad had returned to his writing. In addition to his teaching career, he was the author of a series of detective novels. But he was plagued by writer's block. Even the action-packed adventures of his main character, Mac Mulvey, seemed blah after the Falconer family's wild ride.

After midnight, Aiden lay in bed, trying to think the shadows back into the corners of the room where they belonged.

You can tell yourself that it's all over; that Mom and Dad are free; that HORUS is gone. But after a while the fear has become part of you, even if there's nothing left to be afraid of.

The headlights on the street outside made the shadows on the wall move. Suddenly, there was a screech of tires, running footsteps on the walk, and a loud crash.

2

The sound of shattered glass was replaced by the howl of the house's security alarm.

Aiden still had split-second reaction time, part of every fugitive's instinct for survival. He was out of bed and running down the stairs before the siren reached full power. At that, he was two steps behind his sister. John and Louise Falconer brought up the rear.

"Stay back!" Mom yelled. "You don't know what's down there—or who!"

At the bottom of the steps, Aiden pulled up short beside Meg. All four Falconers stared at the center of their living room. There, in the wreckage of the picture window, sat a cement brick.

Dad, who was wearing hard-soled slippers, crunched through the glass shards. Using a piece of ripped curtain to protect possible evidence, he reached down and picked up the chunk of concrete. Written across its gray surface in stark black Magic Marker was a single word: PAYBACK.

Officer Kincannin regarded the smashed window and hefted the brick experimentally in his hand. "Vandalism."

"Vandalism?" echoed John Falconer. "Look what it says. This act was directed at our family because of who we are."

"It's still a brick through a window," the officer reasoned. "That's vandalism."

"It's a pattern of harassment," Dad argued. "Abusive phone calls, nasty notes stuffed in our mailbox, and now this. The perpetrators get more daring with each incident. What's next—a fire bomb?"

"We're citizens of this town," Mom put in. "Innocent people who need protection. There are two children living in this house."

The officer cocked an eyebrow. "From what I've heard, your kids can look after themselves."

Aiden winced. It was true that he and Meg had shown incredible daring during their time as fugitives. *But that was when we were desperate, running for our lives with nothing to lose. Now everything is supposed to be back to normal. We're trying to be kids again. . . .*

Dad folded his arms in front of him. "Are you going to help us or not?"

Kincannin shrugged. "We can maybe put an extra squad car in the area."

"How about stationing an officer to watch our house?" Mom demanded.

He shook his head. "Not enough manpower. I'll have dispatch ask the cruisers to swing by a few times a night, keep an eye on the place. Best I can do."

Later, as Aiden and his father taped plastic sheeting over the gaping hole in the window, Aiden asked, "Do you think that officer was telling the truth? Are there really not enough cops, or was he just sticking it to us because of who we are?"

"I think he's probably on the level," Dad told him. "It's just a local force, after all."

"So there's nothing we can do?"

"There's one other possibility." John Falconer took a deep breath. "The FBI."

Aiden knew his father wouldn't consider contacting the Bureau unless he was really worried. The FBI had arrested the Falconers in the first place, and then hounded their children across the country. True, the feds had come through for them eventually. But that could never erase a mountain of bitterness and resentment.

"You mean"—Aiden could barely bring himself to speak the name aloud — "Agent Harris?"

"What?" Meg's voice cried from the kitchen. She stormed into the hall to confront them. "Harris? J. Edgar Giraffe?"

"He could get us protection," Dad pointed out.

"I'd rather stay up all night, guarding the house with my toenail clippers," Meg said with conviction.

"He worked pretty hard to get Mom and Dad out of jail at the end," Aiden offered grudgingly.

"Yeah, after putting them there in the first place. That guy *ruined* us, Aiden. Then he chased us for seven thousand miles."

And we're still running, Aiden thought.

3

Aiden moved through the halls of his high school like a zombie. It was just so hard to *care* about English and math and geography now. Like the friendship with Richie that had once been so important to him, classes, grades, even getting into a good college were no more than fluff to the new Aiden.

Life on the run had been horrible, but everything had been incredibly urgent and meaningful. They did what had to be done to survive. It was all that mattered in the world. What was macramé compared to that?

It's the class I'm failing, that's what.

Each day, he'd sit on the bus, fiddling with his snarl of twine, trying to will it into the shape of a plant hanger.

"Forget it, bro," Meg advised. "You're capital-H Hopeless."

"I don't see you acing seventh grade," he retorted.

She regarded him earnestly. "Can you sit through a whole class? I can't anymore. When we were fugitives, we were like jack-in-the-boxes, coiled up under pressure, ready to fly. Well, I'm *still* that way. But in school, all they want you to do is sit still and listen to some boring teacher."

Aiden nodded. "Why do you think Richie hates my guts? It's not everybody else who changed. It's us."

"Sometimes I almost think that other life made more sense," Meg admitted.

"Trust me, it didn't," her brother assured her. "This is perfect by comparison."

But it didn't feel like that.

How long would this go on? They'd been back at school for a month and a half. Surely things should be getting easier by now. Were he and Meg doomed to be outcasts and misfits forever?

An image of the brick appeared in his mind. PAYBACK, the message had said. Maybe that was exactly right. This was punishment for Mom and Dad helping HORUS. Innocent or not, they *had* done it. They'd been tricked into it, but their work had aided terrorists.

At least there's no HORUS anymore.

Richie Pembleton was one of the handful of kids who got off at the Falconers' stop. For at least the twentieth time, Aiden felt the impulse to talk to his old friend, to set things right between them.

But what for? he reflected glumly. *We've got nothing in common anymore. I'm not the kid who built that Foucault pendulum. I'd give anything to change that, but I can't.*

He put his head down and swallowed his words of greeting. Richie did likewise, the brim of his Greenville Cubs hat concealing whatever he might be thinking.

Richie and the others headed straight into the new subdivision. Aiden and Meg were alone as they followed the path that led past the condo development to the older part of the neighborhood.

A battered white van was idling slowly along the road as if searching for an address. Meg pointed at the sign stenciled on its side: WILLIS EXTERMINATING. "Oh, gross — I hope they aren't looking for our house. It could have mice after standing empty for so long."

Aiden nodded grimly. "It could have *gazelles* after standing empty for so long." That would be just their luck. Despised *and* infested.

All at once, the van came to life, bald tires burning rubber. It lurched toward them, closing the distance in two breathless seconds. The front tires jumped the curb, and the vehicle squealed into a tight quarter-turn, blocking their path.

It happened with such astonishing speed that Aiden could only stand and gape. The sliding door was thrown open, and out burst a man dressed entirely in black. A rubber Spider-Man mask covered his head. He was upon Meg in an instant. Roughly, he took hold of her shirt collar. A huge gloved hand covered her nose and mouth with a handkerchief. Meg struggled for a moment before her body went limp, and she sagged in her attacker's arms.

Chloroform! The thought jolted Aiden into action. The only weapon at his disposal was his macramé project. With a cry of *"Let her go!"* he sprang at the assailant, wrapping the plant hanger around Spider-Man's neck and yanking hard.

The man rasped his outrage, but he released Meg, who slumped to the ground. Aiden hung off the black-clad back, pulling on the tough yarn with all his strength.

A second figure—slimmer, and wearing a Mickey Mouse mask—jumped out of the van. He picked Meg up under her arms and began to drag her inside.

"No-o!!" Aiden bellowed.

The lapse in concentration cost him. His opponent bent double, throwing the smaller Aiden up and over his shoulders in a midair somersault. Aiden hit the sidewalk with a jolt. Dazed and helpless, he watched in horror as his sister was stuffed inside the van.

The gravity of the situation came crashing down on him. A vehicle lying in wait. An unprovoked attack on a deserted walkway. Brutal assailants who hid their faces.

This was a kidnapping!

The realization electrified him to the core, clearing the cobwebs from his brain.

Spider-Man advanced menacingly. Aiden rolled away to the right and scrambled to his feet. He snatched a potted geranium from the half-wall surrounding the condo complex and flung it at the mask. The assailant managed to duck the pot, but plant and dirt flew in his eyes. He swore in fury and barked, "Help me!"

Mickey Mouse emerged from the van and moved to join the battle.

It dawned on Aiden: *Why am I fighting in silence?* He and Meg weren't fugitives anymore. They had nothing to fear from attracting attention.

"Help!!" he bellowed at the top of his lungs. *"Call the police! They've got my sister!"*

Spider-Man reached for him with the chloroform-soaked cloth, but Aiden ducked out of the way, still howling for help.

A window opened in the condo complex, and a man shouted, "Hey!"

The van backed up and wheeled around. Aiden could see the driver, who was also wearing a mask — a caricature of golfer Tiger Woods. "Leave him!" ordered a woman's voice.

"Give us a minute!" Spider-Man shouted over his shoulder.

"People are calling the cops, you idiot!" the driver snapped. "We've got the girl. Get in the truck!"

Aiden was still ducking and weaving when the two assailants piled into the van and pulled the door shut. With a screech of tires, the vehicle roared off down the street.

The attack was over. He was free.

But they had taken Meg.

4

Aiden flew down the road in a full sprint, chasing after the exterminators' van that held his little sister. He tried to shout, "*Call nine-one-one!*" but found he had no breath for anything but speed. In the fog of his heart-pounding effort, he almost tripped over a silver Razor scooter lying on the curb in front of number 14. Barely slowing down, he snatched it up and hopped on. It wasn't exactly a pursuit vehicle. Yet anything that could make him faster had to be tried.

He pumped madly with his right foot and was amazed at the amount of acceleration that came immediately. In the farthest reaches of his mind, he knew that the real Aiden Falconer would have been scared witless to be on this glorified roller skate. It took skill, balance, athletic ability, and confidence—all qualities he rarely thought of himself as having. But with Meg in the van, being spirited farther and farther away from him, it was worth the risk of breaking every bone in his body.

The kidnappers were pulling away, weaving in and out

of the light traffic. The van blew through the stop sign at the end of the block and turned left onto the main road.

He was losing her.

The fact that the van was out of sight lent his feet wings. He kicked frantically at the pavement, amping the scooter up to incredible speed. As he approached the corner, the wind roaring in his ears, he peered down the main road, combing the town for a glimpse of the white van. There it was, passing the fire station. So intent was he on following its progress, that it didn't occur to him until the last second —

How do you turn this crazy thing?

He twisted his midsection, hoping the scooter would respond likewise. It did, but not fast enough. He careened full tilt toward the busy intersection.

Should he jump off? It was better than being flattened by a truck.

But then Meg would be gone! So many times the Falconer siblings had risked everything for each other. No way was Aiden going to stop now.

Breathing a silent prayer, he yanked on the handlebars with all his might and leaned left. Horns blared as he barreled through the intersection in a wide turn across four lanes of traffic. With a lurch, he bumped up onto the opposite sidewalk, scattering pedestrians in all directions. With his eyes fixed on the van three blocks ahead, he never saw the movers. Two men unloaded a large padded sofa and started across the walkway to the furniture store. Aiden slammed into the brocade upholstery at thirty miles an hour. The impact stopped him cold, knocking him flat on his back to the pavement. The scooter kept on going until it made violent contact with a mailbox.

Both movers dropped the couch and went down on their hands and knees beside him. "Kid, are you okay?"

Aiden shook off the collision and scrambled to his feet, staring frantically beyond the sofa. There was no white van in sight.

"Call the police," he replied in a reedy voice.

Meg was gone.

Agent Emmanuel Harris leaned back in his brand-new swivel chair, luxuriating in the comfort. The FBI had finally approved his requisition for extra-large office furniture. At six feet seven, he definitely counted as extra large. Now if only they could do something about the rancid coffee . . .

There was an electronic beep, and the computer on his desk clicked out of screen saver. He swiveled the monitor to face him. One of his keywords must have come up. The FBI system automatically scanned all crime reports from around the globe for certain terms and/or names. As the monitor came into focus, he squinted to see which of his search parameters had generated a hit.

FALCONER.

He felt his lunch rising in his stomach, a process helped along by the bad coffee. His least favorite subject — the biggest blunder of his career. He was the agent who had arrested John and Louise Falconer. He considered it entirely his fault that two innocent people had done hard time in prison and that their children had been turned into desperate fugitives.

Hammond, Md.: 3:47 P.M. Margaret Falconer, 11, abducted after disembarking from school bus. Police seeking white van marked "WILLIS EXTERMINATING," last seen heading west. 3 suspects, 2 male, 1 female, wearing novelty masks. Victim daughter of John and Louise Falconer, recently released from . . .

Shock tore him away from the screen. After everything that had happened to them already, now their daughter had been kidnapped?

He strode out of his office, his long legs propelling

him through the halls at impressive speed. This was not his case, not his problem. Yet he was involved as surely as if his boss had dropped the file on his desk. *His* mistake had brought the Falconers into the public eye, and that notoriety had made them targets.

Meg's kidnapping was on his head.

5

Meg returned to awareness through a dense fog and a pounding headache.

"Aiden?"

A gruff voice, definitely not Aiden's, ordered, "Lie still."

She blinked and squinted.

Why can't I see? Am I blind?

No, she could make out light, but no detail. A whiff of laundry detergent tickled her nose. There was something over her head. A sheet? A pillowcase? She tried to reach up and remove it but found that both of her wrists were bound.

Memory came flooding back: walking home from the bus, the exterminators' truck, a burly figure in a Spider-Man mask. He had covered her face with a cloth, damp and strong smelling.

Have I been kidnapped?

The thought was terrifying—but not as terrifying as it should have been. An ordinary eleven-year-old girl would have fallen to pieces, but Meg was hardly ordinary.

Her mind instantly recognized the peril and activated a hidden reserve of experience — the lessons learned during two months as a fugitive.

She took stock of herself. Her hands were tied; her legs were free. She was in a moving vehicle — the exterminators' van?

"Who are you?" she demanded. "What do you want?"

The gruff voice again: "Behave yourself and you won't get hurt."

"Where are you taking me?"

Another voice, a woman's, said, "There it is."

Meg felt the van slow and turn. The wheels crunched on gravel and stopped. The sliding door clattered open.

"Take her legs."

Rough hands grasped her under the arms and by the ankles, hoisting her up and out. She shook her right leg free, reared back, and slammed her sneaker into something soft. There was a loud *oof* as the kidnapper dropped her feet to the ground. In a single motion, she twisted her upper body free and attempted to break into a blind sprint.

Wham! She ran face-first into a cement wall. The impact was so jarring that she fell backward into her captors' waiting hands. She struggled but could not free herself.

"Very stupid, Margaret," the woman told her. "Tie her legs, too."

Meg was lifted again and loaded into another vehicle—a car, she guessed. *It feels like I'm lower down. I must be lying across the floor of the backseat.* She could tell from the hump in the center. Her ankles were bound, although not as tightly as her wrists. The car was started, and soon they were driving again.

Her mind raced. This was crazy! Kidnapped? By who? Why?

She didn't have to stretch for the answer. There were plenty of Falconer haters around, from the vandal who'd thrown a brick through their window to her own middle-school principal.

She set her jaw. *I didn't get Mom and Dad out of prison so I could disappear and never see them again!*

She had to escape. The question was how. The kidnappers had her trussed up like a turkey, not to mention sightless. Her nose throbbed painfully where she had connected with the wall, and she tasted blood. Another collision like that and she wouldn't have to worry about her captors harming her. She'd be doing a pretty good job of it by herself.

There's no way to make a run for it if I can't see where I'm going. But by the time I fight my way out of this pillowcase, they'll just grab me. . . .

What could she do?

Amazingly, her thoughts turned to Mac Mulvey, the hero of Dad's novels. Aiden was the big Mac Mulvey fan; Meg didn't like the wild, exaggerated action. Still, she couldn't deny that ideas from Mulvey's adventures had saved the Falconer kids more than once during their weeks on the run.

Secretly, Meg had begun to give the novels a second chance. The stories were pure cheese, but Mulvey certainly spent plenty of time tied up by a variety of enemies.

Maybe something from the books can work for me. . . .

When blindfolded, Mulvey relied on his keen sense of hearing. Meg listened, tuning out the engine noise of the car. Three voices — three kidnappers! They were mostly complaining about bad drivers and less traffic lights.

All at once, she remembered *Diamonds Are a Wiseguy's Best Friend*. Mulvey was able to escape by using his foot to open the door of the hit man's Cadillac. Of course, the Caddy had been doing ninety — another example of why Dad's books were totally unbelievable. Nobody could survive a jump at that speed. But this car was on city streets with lots of stops. The fall wouldn't hurt her.

Her ankles were bound, so she moved both feet together, probing for the door handle.

"Sit tight!" the gruff kidnapper growled from the front.

"The hump is digging into my side," she protested.

"I'm all broken up about that." Pure sarcasm.

"Here — I'll help you." This voice was also male, but younger and kinder. It must have belonged to the third captor, the one in the backseat with her. He supported her shoulders, enabling her to rotate a quarter turn onto her back. As she twisted into a more comfortable position, she felt her left sneaker lodge behind something hard. The handle!

"Thanks," she said aloud. "That's better." Inside she was thinking: *This is it!*

She waited until the car was stopped at yet another light. Then she pulled with her toes until she felt the handle click and kicked the door open. In a single motion, she hurled herself at the door.

"Hey — !"

She wasn't sure which kidnapper said it — possibly all three. It didn't matter. There was no turning back now.

She was *out* — her feet were, anyway. Someone grabbed her tightly around the waist.

No — not when I'm so close. . . .

She squirmed against the hold, but more arms latched onto her, and she was wrenched inside. The door slammed.

The gruff voice growled, "We're lucky no one was around. We can't have that happen again. Put her out."

A moment later, the cinch of her hood loosened, and a meaty hand was reaching up at her, pushing a white cloth. She twisted to avoid the overpowering fumes, but the chloroform was forced over her nose and mouth, and consciousness was receding.

. . . not a hallucination . . . really happening . . .

And her last thought before everything went dark: *Mom and Dad won't be able to handle this.*

6

Aiden peered out through the drawn curtains at what used to be his front lawn. A full-fledged media circus surrounded the Falconer house. There were reporters, camera crews, sound engineers. A fleet of TV news mobile units clogged the quiet street, satellite dishes reaching for the sky.

He could barely bring himself to accept that it was happening again. This kind of press firestorm had been unleashed on the family once before. The attention had been so intense that Aiden and Meg had been yanked from a series of foster homes and placed on an isolated juvenile prison farm just to avoid the spotlight.

This was worse, Aiden decided. *Mom and Dad's trial was awful, but at least we knew they were alive. With Meg . . .*

No, he couldn't think about that—his sister, under the total control of her captors. If they meant to kill her, there would be nothing anyone could do to prevent it.

Aiden couldn't stand to see his confident father so helpless. Dad had actually allowed the local police chief to talk him into making a statement for the mob outside.

Aiden intercepted his father at the door. "Dad — don't do it!" he whispered. "It's a feeding frenzy! They don't care about Meg — they just want you and Mom crying on TV!"

His father looked torn in two. "But the chief says we have to get the word out — "

"The word *is* out," Aiden insisted. "All these reporters wouldn't be here if it wasn't."

Chief Aberfeldy brushed him off and took Dr. Falconer's arm. "Come on, John. My guys have set up a microphone on the porch."

"I'm going with you," Aiden said determinedly. If he couldn't prevent his father from making this mistake, at least he could supply moral support. He glanced back at his mother, who was collapsed on the couch, an expression of disbelief on her pale features. At least she wasn't taking part in this freak show. They stepped outside.

It was twice as bad as Aiden had imagined. The pandemonium of shouted questions was an uninterrupted roar. What seemed like thousands of camera flashes made the crowd seem to sparkle. There was even some heckling and boos from the ever-present Falconer haters, who still believed Mom and Dad were traitors.

Chief Aberfeldy's pleas for order were lost at first in the cacophony. Dad struggled to communicate his message—that the public should watch for anyone matching Meg's description.

Amid the chaos, Aiden's eyes fell on the figure of a very tall man bulling his way through the throng. Coffee sloshed out of his extra-large travel mug as he was jostled, but his progress was steady. There was no mistaking this new presence. It was a face straight out of the Falconer family's darkest moments.

Agent Emmanuel Harris.

With a single sweep of his arm, he gestured Dr. Falconer, Aiden, and the chief away from the microphone, and faced the media.

He was recognized instantly. He was known to the press, and, at six feet seven, impossible to mistake.

"Agent Harris, do you have a statement from the FBI?"

"Yes," Harris said shortly. "Get lost. Leave this yard, or I'll have you removed."

A babble of angry protest rose from the crowd.

"You can't kick us off the street!" piped up somebody.

"No," Harris agreed. "But I can kick you *into* the street. This yard is private property, and that *will* be enforced."

To Aiden's amazement, the media swarm began a reluctant and disorganized retreat, with the police showing them the way.

"They'll just start using more powerful lenses," grunted Harris, ushering Aiden and his father back inside. To Aberfeldy, he added, "That doesn't mean we have to perform for them like trained seals."

At the sight of the towering FBI agent, Louise Falconer leaped to her feet. "You! They assigned *you* to this case?"

Harris addressed himself to all three Falconers. "I'm sorry to hear what's happened to Meg. I promise to do everything in my power to get her home in one piece."

"You've done enough already," Dad said coldly. "Do you think those kidnappers would have heard of our daughter if it weren't for you?"

The agent didn't argue the point. "You don't like me. It's understandable, and I accept it. But we're going to have to find a way to work together."

"Let's go in the kitchen," Mom suggested. She had no great love for Emmanuel Harris, but nothing was more important to her than the safety of her family. "We can talk there."

Aiden followed his parents and Harris through the door and froze. A strange man sat at the table, pounding the keyboard of a notebook computer.

Dad pulled up short. "Who are you?"

The newcomer looked up and beamed at them. "I'm Rufus Sehorn." He said it as if he were a dear family friend, not an uninvited intruder.

Harris clamped a meaty hand on his shoulder. "What are you doing in this house?"

Sehorn scowled at him. "Why are you so worried about *me* in the house? Why would they let *you* in the house, after the suffering you've caused this family?"

"Do we know you?" asked Mom in confusion.

"Not yet, but you will." He shook himself free of Harris and hefted a large bag. "I brought Dunkin' Donuts."

The FBI man was growing angry. "I don't care if you brought a shipment of gold bars. You're trespassing."

"Just waiting for an invite," Sehorn amended. "I'm the Blog Hog. That's my Web site—*bloghog.usa*. News, opinions, and whatnot. The whatnot was my idea. All the blogs have news and opinions, but mine is the only one with whatnot."

In spite of the tense situation, Aiden almost smiled. Rufus Sehorn reminded Aiden of a hobbit, minus the furry feet. The blogger was short and slight, with a fresh-faced, wide-eyed earnestness that seemed to radiate openness and honesty.

Harris was not as charmed. "The press has already been removed, and that includes you," he said hotly. "You have no idea the kind of anguish these people are going through."

"Don't I?" Sehorn swiveled his laptop to face them. "Read my latest posting."

The Falconers crowded around the small screen.

I'm sitting in the kitchen of Doctors John and Louise Falconer, who have just heard the news that their eleven-year-old daughter has been kidnapped. Once imprisoned as America's most notorious traitors, today they are free—and also not free, thanks to a press that has cursed them with everlasting fame and everlasting suspicion. That same media besieges their comfortable home today, where John, Louise, and their teenage son, Aiden, snack on Dunkin' Donuts, for there is no belly for cooking within such a state of fear. They eat, though they taste not a single bite, awaiting word from the kidnappers. And mostly they pray. . . .

"They're not eating doughnuts," Harris pointed out sourly. "You are."

John Falconer addressed the blogger. "What do you want?"

"I want to help," Sehorn replied readily. "Even though you're out of jail, a lot of people still don't accept your innocence. We can turn that around."

"How?" asked Aiden.

"By telling your story on my Web site. I believe that things will go better for Margaret if you're not the bogeymen anymore. A sympathetic public might convince her captors to let her go. Or the extra attention could produce tips that lead to her rescue. I can make that happen — if you'll let me."

"All right, that's enough," the agent interrupted. "Get out of this house or I'll run you in for breaking and entering."

"No." Louise Falconer indicated the laptop. "This one paragraph shows more understanding than we've ever seen from the FBI. We'll do this interview. We'll do whatever it takes to bring Meg home."

"You'll have approval over every word before I post it on the site," the Blog Hog assured her.

Harris took a swig of cold coffee and reached for a doughnut. "But when the interview's over, you're *gone,* got it?"

The pastries tasted like sawdust, even though Aiden was starving. He was too anxious to eat. If this interview really was the key to saving Meg, they had to get every word exactly right.

But deep down, he had a sinking feeling that nothing so important was ever so simple.

7

Meg paced the room like a penned animal.

Some room, she thought in disgust. More like a concrete box, lit with a bare bulb inside a metal protective cage. Shadows of the cage were cast over every surface — images of bars, fences, captivity.

The only thing missing is barbed wire. . . .

This was a prison cell, and there was no way out.

The space was empty except for a pile of wooden shipping pallets in one corner. The skids were half rotted by long exposure to damp air. The walls, floor, and ceiling weren't in much better shape — ancient and crumbling. Whatever this place was, it hadn't been occupied in a very long time.

At least she could see again. The kidnappers had untied her wrists and ankles before literally tossing her into her prison. She'd ripped the pillowcase off her head just in time to catch a glimpse of the Spider-Man mask disappearing behind the heavy steel door. That made sense. He belonged to the gruff voice and seemed to be the muscles of the operation. He was good at it, too. She rubbed her hip, which throbbed in pain where it had made contact with the cement floor.

She looked around. What was this place? The only feature was a narrow horizontal window high above her at ceiling level. Could this be a basement? That would certainly explain the dank chill and moldy smell. But the basement of what?

She peered at the window. It was scratched and dirty, and the sharp angle made it difficult to see outside.

A sudden click made her jump. The door swung open and in stepped the smaller kidnapper — the one in the Mickey Mouse mask. Fearfully, Meg backed up a few steps. There was nowhere to run in this concrete dungeon — and nothing she could use to defend herself.

Mickey Mouse held out a McDonald's bag. "You must be hungry."

She had thought this might be the woman, but the voice was male. It was the younger-sounding man, the one who'd been kind to her in the backseat of the car.

"What do you want from me?"

"Don't get excited. Nobody's going to hurt you."

"You've already hurt me," she accused. "It feels like someone took a sledgehammer to my head."

"That's just the chloroform," Mickey Mouse explained. "We don't mean you any harm. We just want — "

Meg pounced on the opening. "You want what?

What's this about? Why have you brought me here?"

The mask hid his expression, but the sudden tension in his shoulders told Meg that he was wary of saying too much.

"Here's your dinner." He set the bag down on the floor. "Maybe some food will cure your headache."

Meg was starving. Yet her every instinct was to take this meal that smelled so tantalizing and throw it right in his face.

But you'll need to keep up your strength if you want to have a chance to escape.

And that was something she intended to do.

She took a step forward, picked up the bag, and looked inside. A Big Mac. She couldn't resist showing a touch of defiance. "I hate the special sauce."

"I usually scrape it off," offered Mickey. He paused. "Is there anything else I can get you?"

"A ride home," Meg replied bitterly.

"Hang in there. We'll get through this." He walked out, snapping the lock into place.

The sheer unfairness of that statement brought tears of frustration to her eyes. *We'll get through this.* Like he was her fellow victim and not one of the perpetrators of this crime.

What did they want? Ransom? One thing was clear—they knew exactly who she was. They knew her name. She wasn't just some random girl they'd snatched. Were they Falconer haters taking revenge on a family they considered traitors? Or was this something else, something Meg hadn't even considered?

Stop it! she ordered herself. *You're kidnapped. It doesn't matter why. All that's important is what happens now.*

It was a lesson she and Aiden had learned on the run. Fugitives had no time for the big picture. All their energy had to be focused on what came next. The next move, the next challenge, the next minute. Often it had come down to seconds.

Her gaze tracked up the crumbling cement to the tiny window. *That* would be next for Meg.

How can I climb a twelve-foot concrete wall in an empty room?

Her eyes fell on the mound of discarded and broken pallets, laced with silvery spiderwebs.

No, not empty. Not empty at all.

The setup resembled a home video game system, like Xbox without the joysticks. Aiden had to remind himself that the equipment had nothing to do with fun and recreation. It was surveillance gear designed to monitor and trace all phone calls to the Falconer home.

"What are you looking at?"

The FBI tech was regarding him over the tangle of wires, a sour expression on his face.

"I was just watching." Aiden was good at science, electronics in particular.

The tech scowled at him. "I've got a tough enough job to do, kid, without you sticking your nose in it. Go break out of jail or something."

Aiden backed up a step. It wasn't his first nasty rebuke from a Falconer hater. But this guy worked for the FBI. Hadn't he noticed that his own agency had found Mom and Dad innocent and dropped all charges against Aiden and Meg, too?

If we have enemies inside the FBI, will they even try to rescue Meg?

It was hard to think of the word "enemy" without associating it with Emmanuel Harris. The six-foot-seven agent was now officially heading up the investigation of Meg's disappearance. How ironic was that? The man who had come within a hair of destroying the Falconer family had been placed in charge of saving it.

Harris was in the kitchen, briefing Mom and Dad, when Aiden entered the room. ". . . and you have to watch what you say to Rufus Sehorn. His background check came up clean, but he's no ordinary reporter. A blogger has no editors, no standards, and no rules." He scrolled through *www.bloghog.usa* on the notebook computer on the table. "Here, for example, where you talk about how good Meg is at cards—"

"Rufus specifically asked for personal details," Louise Falconer explained coldly. "We're trying to humanize Meg. To humanize the whole family, really, to undo some of the damage that's been done to our reputation."

"That's fine," Harris said patiently, "but you have to use common sense. When the kidnappers see 'card player,' they might conclude that Meg has an exceptional memory—maybe even a photographic memory. That would make it harder for them to release her. They'd be afraid she'd remember something that might help the police track them down."

Mom uttered a cry of pain, as if she'd been slapped.

Aiden tried to soothe his mother. "Come on, how could you be expected to think of that when Meg's been kidnapped?"

Dad shook his head. "What kind of criminologists are we? Failing our own daughter."

"No one's failed anybody yet," Harris reminded them. "Let's just be extra careful around a blogger. There's an awful lot riding on what we do."

Aiden spoke up. "Has anybody spotted the exterminators' van?"

Harris nodded. "Bethesda PD found it abandoned in an alley. No fingerprints except your sister's."

"The kidnappers must have been wearing gloves," Dad mused.

"If the van was in Bethesda," Aiden challenged, "why aren't you searching every house in town?"

"We think Bethesda was just a transfer point," the agent informed them. "There were tire tracks under the gravel next to the abandoned van. Our crime scene people are checking it out. Looks like a car, not a van or SUV, probably GM or Chrysler. We've modified the alert."

"But that's half the cars on the road!" Aiden protested. "By the time you find the right one, Meg could be . . ." His voice trailed off.

"I know it's not much," Harris admitted, "but it's all

we've got right now. At least till there's a ransom demand, or some kind of direct message from the kidnappers."

"What if they don't want ransom?" Mom asked. "What if they want a dead Falconer? Remember, they tried to take Aiden, too—" She was trying to stay professional, but the shakiness of her voice gave her away.

"I almost wish they *had* gotten me," Aiden said hoarsely. "Not that I want to be kidnapped. I just hate that Meg's all alone. We were kind of good together. You know, in tough spots."

"That's nothing to celebrate," Dad scolded. "No child should ever have to endure what you and your sister did." He cast a scorching look at Harris.

"Let's just keep our heads," the agent advised. "For Meg's sake."

For Meg's sake.

Magic words, thought Aiden. They had the power to make the Falconer family cooperate with the hated Emmanuel Harris.

9

Meg stepped back to survey her handiwork. One of the wooden pallets was propped up at an angle beneath the small window. Another stood on top of it, extending like a ladder to the narrow opening. This wobbly arrangement was anchored in place by four more skids, laid out across the floor, braced against the opposite wall.

It wasn't pretty. But would it get the job done?

She placed a foot on one of the slats and was genuinely amazed that the entire mess didn't collapse like a house of cards under her weight. Encouraged, she hoisted herself to the higher skid. This was a much more precarious balance, since it stood nearly flat against the wall.

She climbed carefully, leaning her weight forward in an attempt to keep the pallet from tipping over backward. The prospect of bashing her brains out on the hard cement wasn't appealing. But the thought that the kidnappers might barge in to investigate the noise of the crash was even worse.

Another shaky foothold. Her outstretched arm was just eighteen inches from the window. Gritting her teeth, she raised a trembling leg to the next rung. The pallet shimmied, and she pressed her shoulder into the wood to keep it in place.

Eight inches separated Meg's hand from the window. One more step. She could make it. She *would* make it.

One . . . two . . . *three*!

Her fingers slapped onto the window ledge. Breathing hard, she hoisted herself to the opening.

Her first close look at the window brought a gasp of disappointment. Security glass—with wire mesh inside the immovable pane. There was no way she could ever get through it.

As her body slumped in defeat, the toe of her sneaker nudged the top of the skid ever so slightly away from the wall. It teetered backward, passing the point of no return.

In a panic, she tried to catch it with a dangling foot and succeeded in wedging her ankle between the slats. The effort twisted her out of position, and she lost her grip on the ledge with her left hand, hanging on doggedly with her right. Her free arm flailed wildly, fingers clamping onto the bars of the protective cage around the light.

Her weight proved too much for the deteriorating ceiling. With a sickening crunch, the crumbling cement gave up its hold on the metal cage.

She was falling.

She sucked back the scream that tried to explode from her throat. The pallet around her ankle hit the floor and smashed into pieces. The force pitched her backward. Her head struck a skid, cracking rotted wood.

Everything went dark.

Sleep.

Aiden snorted into his pillow. Yeah, right. Like *that* was going to happen.

It had been Harris's advice as he'd headed out the door. "Get some sleep."

"You're leaving?" Aiden had exclaimed in disbelief. "But there's no news—no progress! What—Meg can only be in danger during work hours?"

"I've got two agents here around the clock," Harris assured him. "Our tech people are monitoring your e-mail accounts in case the kidnappers try to contact you that way. We're covered."

Reluctantly, Aiden had to admit it made sense. Even on the run, the Falconer kids had found time for rest. It had been the only way for them to stay sharp. The FBI couldn't rescue Meg if they were too exhausted to function.

He had finally drifted into an uneasy slumber when the shouting started.

Heart thumping, he scrambled to the window. Squinting in the darkness, he could just make out one of the FBI men wrestling with an unknown assailant near the front bushes.

The kidnappers? Have they come back for me? It made no sense, and yet . . .

The door burst open and another agent ran onto the scene. The glint of metal was unmistakable. A gun!

"Freeze!"

As the intruder stopped struggling, the light coming from inside fell on his Greenville Cubs baseball cap.

Aiden sprinted for the stairs.

His pajama-clad father grabbed him on the first landing.

"It's Richie!" Aiden exclaimed.

"At midnight?"

"That's high noon for him — remember?"

Richie's parents both worked nights, turning their son into the ultimate night owl. He'd memorized every late-late-show science fiction movie word for word. The kid was fluent in Klingon. He used to show up at all hours, calling Aiden by bouncing pebbles off his window. That had probably been Richie's plan tonight before the feds pounced on him.

Dad strode for the door, Aiden hot on his heels. "Don't shoot! It's my son's friend!"

By the time they reached the scene, poor Richie was flat on his face in the grass, his hands cuffed tightly behind his back.

Between them, the two Falconers managed to convince their FBI protectors that the intruder was harmless.

"Sorry, kid," apologized the agent who unlocked the shackles. "But you've got to admit that most people skulking outside a house at midnight have nothing good in mind. Especially this house."

Richie nodded meekly.

Maybe now he'll understand why I can't go back to being his old buddy, Aiden reflected, leading Richie inside. *This is my life now—cops and guns.*

"Don't stay up too late," Dad advised them before heading upstairs. "This isn't the time for a slumber party."

Aiden pushed his friend into a kitchen chair and cracked open two bottles of water. "You okay, Rich?"

Richie took a long drink. "How'd you know it was me?"

Aiden cast him a ghost of a smile. "Because the Greenville Cubs only have one fan." It faded quickly. "You can't hang around here, Rich. We've got serious trouble."

"Your sister. It was on the late news. I came as soon as I heard. Who would kidnap Meg? Do you think it's the group that framed your parents?"

Aiden shrugged helplessly. "They're all either dead or

in jail. But there are plenty of people who hate us out there. I really don't want to talk about it."

"What can I do to help?" Richie asked earnestly.

For some reason, this offer of assistance actually made Aiden feel worse. "Nothing," he mumbled.

Richie wouldn't take no for an answer. "Just say the word. Even if it's as simple as picking up your homework until all this is over."

Until all this is over. That simple phrase underscored the huge chasm that had opened up between Aiden and his friend. To Richie, *until all this is over* referred to a time when this situation was resolved, and life could go on.

To Aiden, it was very different.

When "all this" was over, Aiden Falconer might very well not have a sister.

10

It was the worst headache Meg could ever remember. With it came double vision, which scared the daylights out of her. When her sight cleared and she recalled where she was, that scared her even more.

The escape attempt. A twelve-foot fall into a pile of wooden skids. Sharp pain and then blackness. How long had she been unconscious? She listened for signs of the kidnappers, waiting for them to burst through the door. Surely they must have heard her fall.

No one came. Well, at least that was something. She could try again. There had to be some way out. . . .

If only her head would stop throbbing!

Aiden had always accused her of having a head like a cannonball. It had probably saved her from a concussion or worse tonight.

She bit her lip. If only Aiden were here to make fun of her.

Aiden. What was he doing right now? Sleeping? She doubted it. If Aiden had been kidnapped, she wouldn't be sleeping. She'd be fighting tooth and nail to track him down.

No, that was fugitive thinking. In those weeks on the run, each had rescued the other countless times. But the Falconers were regular citizens again. Regular citizens didn't take the law into their own hands. They called the police.

Were the police looking for her? Would they care about the disappearance of one of the notorious Falconers? And even if they did give it their best, how would they ever find her in this basement dungeon, lying in a pile of splintered wood, crumbled concrete and plaster, and shattered glass?

Glass? Why glass?

Then she saw the filament from the broken light-bulb.

I must have pulled the fixture clean off when I grabbed hold of the cage.

She frowned. That bulb was the only light, and it lay in shards all around her. So why wasn't it dark in here?

Slowly and painfully, she tilted her aching head to look up at the ceiling. Sure enough, the light was coming from above. But its source was not in the basement. It was shining down from the room upstairs through a hole the size of a car tire. When she'd pulled the fixture down, a good chunk of the ceiling had come with it.

Without even knowing it, she had ripped herself the ultimate escape route! That was ground level. From there, surely she could make her way to an exit—one that wasn't locked and guarded.

It had taken her nearly an hour to arrange the pallets so that she could reach to the window. She had everything back in place in a few minutes. Who knew how much precious time she had wasted lying unconscious?

The trick would be to get from the window to the opening in the ceiling without another disastrous fall. Careful to keep her makeshift ladder in balance, Meg climbed up the skids until she had both hands on the window ledge. The hole to freedom was about four feet away, directly behind her. Craning her neck, she searched for some sort of handhold in the concrete above. Nothing.

There was only one way to get this done, Meg told herself with a sinking heart. She would have to jump for it and hope for the best.

She swung her legs back, which only had the effect of knocking away the pallet she'd been standing on. Now she was hanging from the window ledge with no way to get down.

That's okay, she thought determinedly. *There's no down for me anymore. Just over, up, and out.*

Wishing that she hadn't quit gymnastics after the second week, she braced both feet against the wall, focusing all her energy into the maneuver she was about to perform. With a mighty heave, she kicked off the wall, twisting her body in a midair one-eighty. She was right underneath the opening, but her upward motion was running out. Gravity was beginning to pull her down.

At the last second, both arms shot up through the jagged opening and clamped onto the floor of the room above.

Oh, no! The cement was still crumbling. She could feel it disintegrating between her fingers. Dust and pebbles rained into her face, choking her. Soon she would be holding nothing but air. Then — a twelve-foot drop. The best she could hope for would be two broken legs.

She closed her eyes and waited for the fall.

It didn't come. Suddenly, she was holding on to something solid — a steel reinforcing rod embedded in the cement.

Meg Falconer was not one to waste a gift. Gasping and spitting, she hauled herself up and scrambled through the opening, coming to rest on a safe portion of the concrete floor above. There she lay, willing her heartbeat to slow down. She had made it this far. But she had to find a way out of the building before she would be free. The kidnappers were around here somewhere.

She had to be far away before they found out she was missing.

She took quick stock of her surroundings. She was in a huge factory area, long abandoned and dotted with debris and derelict equipment. There were enormous windows on three sides, high up. All she could see outside was the bricks of neighboring buildings and the darkness of night. The exit was nowhere to be found.

Come on, there's got to be a way out of here!

She ran to what must have been the loading bay with its heavy metal garage door. She tried the hanging control. This place clearly had electricity — the lights worked. But the button required a key. And the door was padlocked.

A faded sign caught her attention: OFFICE. Her spirits soared. Surely, the office had its own exit to the street. The secretaries and bosses wouldn't have come in through the plant.

She threw the door open and entered a narrow hall, edging along a corridor that was piled high on both sides with stacked chairs. There seemed to be several offices. All she could do was pick one and hope for the best.

Her first choice turned out to be a large storage closet that led nowhere. She tried another door.

This room was occupied. A woman was asleep on an old threadbare couch. On the floor beside her lay a bear of a man with a dark, bushy beard, also deep in slumber. The third member of the group was a slim young man of perhaps nineteen or twenty. He was very much awake and sat watching a soccer match on a small handheld TV.

Meg was so stressed out and frazzled that it took a moment before the realization kicked in.

She was looking at her kidnappers.

11

The delay proved costly. The young man leaped up with a shout that woke the other two.

A detonation of pure adrenaline galvanized Meg into action. By sheer instinct, she tipped over one of the chair stacks, blocking the doorway with the resulting pileup. She ran down the hall, upending more stacks, leaving a jumble of furniture in her wake.

Angry shouts filled the corridor behind her, along with the crash of metal and plastic. The kidnappers were on her tail, struggling to bulldoze through the obstacle course.

Meg kept on going, wheeling around the corner. Dead ahead was another office, this one with a cluttered old desk and — was that a window? She could see it more clearly as she ran toward it, still scattering chairs at her heels. The glass was gone, and a sheet of corrugated cardboard was duct-taped to the frame.

She knew she was going to jump. Even if there was a bed of nails submerged in a bathtub of acid on the other side of that window, it was preferable to spending another minute in here.

She blasted through the doorway, vaulted onto the desk, and dove headfirst into the cardboard. It broke apart on impact, and she was catapulted out onto a cement sidewalk. She tucked and rolled, trying to minimize injury. In truth, she barely noticed the pain. She was out!

No sooner was she back on her feet than something tripped her up, dropping her to the pavement again. The shock of going down when she believed herself scot-free brought tears to her eyes.

What is this—some kind of booby trap? Were they expecting me to make a run for it?

She squinted in the darkness and spotted the wire that had toppled her. It was a cable extending through the transom above her escape window right to the transformer box at the edge of the sidewalk.

So that was how the kidnappers were bringing electricity to an abandoned building.

She grabbed the wire and yanked it from the box. The warehouse went dark behind her, but she didn't wait around to see it. She was already in full flight, screaming, "Help! *Help!*"

How much of a head start had the stunt with the

chairs and pulling the plug bought her? It was impossible to tell.

Not enough, she thought grimly.

"Help! Help me!"

She scanned the area, dismay swelling inside her. Where were the people? The houses? The cars? The streets were deserted. The only buildings were old warehouses and industrial structures. Everything was dark.

"Help me! I've been kidnapped! Somebody! Anybody!"

No response. Nothing. Not even the sound of distant traffic.

Where was this place? The moon?

She stopped shouting, concentrating all her energy on running. Who knew how far she'd have to go before she found another living soul, someone who could call the police for her?

And then she heard another living soul—in the form of running feet behind her. She risked a quick glance over her shoulder.

It was *them*! The bearded one and the young guy were sprinting up the street, closing the gap fast.

Meg turned on the jets, knees pumping like pistons. She was still losing ground. Athletic as she was, her legs were shorter, her lung capacity smaller.

Desperately, she searched left and right for an alley

to duck down, a fence to squeeze through — anywhere she'd fit but her pursuers wouldn't.

I didn't come this far just to get recaptured!

Suddenly, a late-model Buick squealed around a corner and veered onto the sidewalk, cutting off her escape. The driver's door burst open, and out jumped the woman Meg had seen asleep in the office — the third kidnapper.

I'm trapped!

She wheeled, streaking across the road. She didn't delude herself — in the next thirty seconds, she would be caught. So this precious half-minute of freedom had to count. Meg had that much time to tell the world that she had been here.

I have to send a message, make a mark, leave a clue. . . .

But how?

When she spotted the gas station, it almost gave her hope. But it was like every other building around here — closed and deserted. With a sinking heart, she realized that what she'd taken as a sign of life had been the sound of two flags flapping in the stiff breeze.

All at once, her brother's words came back to her, echoing in her head: *People get crazy about flags.*

Could this be a way to send up an SOS? It was a long shot, but the only shot she had. With the kidnappers closing in on her, she made a beeline for the station's twin flagpoles. Picking up a broken piece of brick, she began to hack at the cleat holding the cord that raised and lowered the first flag. It was a lot stronger than the one she had broken by accident at school. But persistent banging eventually knocked it loose. The cord sang as the Stars and Stripes dropped to the pavement.

She turned her attention to the second pole and started working on that cleat. Her pursuers were so close that she could actually feel the vibration of their footfalls.

Come on—break! Break!

The bearded man was almost upon her. "Drop it!"

Determinedly, Meg brought the brick down with deadly force. The cleat flew off, clattering across the asphalt. The flag of the Commonwealth of Virginia hit the ground a second later.

Meg wielded the brick gamely, ready to do battle despite the David-versus-Goliath odds. To her shock, she was disarmed from behind.

"Don't even think about it, Margaret," the woman said firmly.

Soon she was in the backseat of the car, sandwiched between the two men.

"Very stupid," the bearded one told her.

Meg was too devastated to reply. A terrible thought occurred to her as the car headed back in the direction of the warehouse. She was no longer being held by impersonal Halloween masks. These were real people, real criminals, and these were their real faces.

She remembered a piece of wisdom from her father's Mac Mulvey novels. When you've seen your kidnappers' faces, it usually means they're going to kill you to keep you from identifying them after your release.

Had Meg Falconer just signed her own death warrant?

12

"**I**'m not going to school! How can I go to school?"

"I know how you feel," John Falconer told his son, "but it's the best thing for all of us if we try to live our lives as normally as possible."

"Dad—listen to yourself!" Aiden pleaded. "Meg's been kidnapped! Nothing is normal till we get her back."

"But until we do," Mom put in, "it's necessary to eat, sleep, and put one foot in front of the other. Bad enough that Dad and I have to sit around here wringing our hands. Who knows how long it'll be before there's a break in the case?"

"This isn't a lesson for your students at the college!" Aiden ranted. "We're talking about *Meg*!"

Emmanuel Harris stepped into the kitchen where the argument was taking place. "Agent Ortiz has the car out front to take Aiden to school."

Aiden turned accusing eyes on his parents. "*He's* in on this with you?"

"Of course," his father confirmed. "You can't go to school without an escort."

"I can't go to school, period!" Aiden snapped. "This is the craziest thing I've ever heard! Do you really think I'm going to learn anything?"

"Be grateful," Harris advised. "You've got something to do. Do it."

"You just want me out of the way," Aiden accused bitterly.

"That, too," the FBI man agreed. "We need to be left alone to do our job. Right now, that job is waiting. You're too jumpy to be any help. Go to school."

And that was that. At the most traumatic point in a life that had already seen more than its share of trauma, Aiden and his FBI escort arrived at Churchill East High School.

His appearance in the student common area created a buzz, sending dozens of hands reaching for cell phones. Meg's kidnapping was front-page news. No one had expected to see her brother the very next day.

They probably think I don't even care.

Agent Ortiz was a nice-enough guy. But he was bald with a bushy mustache, so he didn't exactly blend in with the student body. He was the absolute stereotype of a bodyguard—sunglasses hiding cold eyes, unsmiling expression, the bulge of a weapon in his breast pocket. His mere presence sucked the air out of a classroom.

As uncomfortable as it was to be shadowed by an agent, Aiden was grateful that his FBI nursemaid held the other curious kids at a distance. Having to talk about Meg, answer questions, and accept sympathy would have been unbearable.

Ortiz kept everybody away—with one exception. Richie Pembleton was determined to be helpful. He tagged along after Aiden and Ortiz all morning, trying to provide aid and comfort . . . but driving Aiden insane.

"You're doing the right thing, man. School's the place for you today. You know what? By the time you get home, Meg could already be there. Maybe she's there this minute. How about I call your house and check?"

Ortiz caught Aiden's eye. "You want me to arrest him?"

Aiden sighed. "Listen, Rich, I appreciate all your—support. But this is a really tough spot. I need to work it out on my own."

"Now you're talking," Richie enthused. "Okay, what do we do first?"

Richie simply would not get the message, nor was Aiden surprised. His friend's stubbornness was legendary. This was a kid who chose to love a baseball team that hadn't had a winning season since the forties, even though they played in some sub-basement minor league no one had ever heard of.

"The pro teams have millions of fans," he'd explained time and time again. "Greenville needs me." And he stuck by his beloved Cubs through thin and thin.

In Richie's mind, this was the same thing. Aiden needed him.

Aiden had no choice but to lay it on the line. "Listen, Rich, no offense, but you've got to go away. I don't want you near me. I don't want *anybody* near me. It's just too hard."

Unbelievable—Meg's life was in danger. The family was fractured again, his parents suffering even more torment. And now he had to carry the guilt for wounding Richie Pembleton.

Shouldn't there be a limit to the number of things I'm supposed to feel bad about?

Classes were a complete waste of time. Meg never left Aiden's mind.

The only bright spot in the day was that Agent Ortiz turned out to be skilled at macramé. But even Aiden's first passing grade in that course was marred by what happened next.

There was a sharp rap at the door of the art room. In

marched Alicia Rangel's father. He cast a dirty look in Aiden's direction, grabbed his daughter by the arm, and announced to the teacher that he was pulling her out of school due to "safety concerns."

Aiden was taken aback. What safety concerns? Alicia wasn't a Falconer. No kidnappers were targeting her.

I'm the safety concern.

If Meg's captors came after Aiden, there could be a shoot-out, stray bullets, a hostage standoff maybe. Who would risk exposing their kid to that?

As it turned out, the Rangels' decision was not unique. All day, a steady stream of cars clogged the circular drive — parents taking their teenagers out of harm's way.

I'm a menace. A walking bull's-eye.

As the afternoon wore on, Aiden gave up on classes altogether. His presence only served to make people uneasy, including the teachers. He spent most of his time in the library, checking *www.bloghog.usa* to see if there were any updates on Meg. The truth was that Aiden trusted Rufus Sehorn's Web site more than the entire FBI. That was pretty crazy, considering that Meg's life was in the Bureau's hands. It would have been laughable if it hadn't been so scary.

Anyway, the Blog Hog had nothing new to report — exactly *because* of the FBI. Emmanuel Harris was keeping a tight lid on information coming out of the Falconer house. It was all for Meg's sake, Harris said, the best chance of getting her back safe and sound. Aiden wasn't so sure. It was hard to accept the word of a man who had already shattered their family once. Mom and Dad had decided to trust Harris. But they were so devastated, were they even thinking straight?

The news blackout was evident in the regular media as well. The library had a television tuned to the local news, but all Aiden saw about his sister was in the scrolling updates:

NO WORD YET FROM KIDNAPPERS WHO ABDUCTED

MARGARET FALCONER — FBI.

Aiden squirmed in his chair as his stomach tightened. It had been on this very monitor that he had watched his parents' arrest by Agent Harris and a SWAT team from Homeland Security. That had been more than a year ago. It felt like yesterday.

Someone on the screen was raving about the decline of patriotism. Aiden wondered when "those Falconer traitors" would come up as an example of how not to love your country. But the man had a different target in mind.

"*. . . and in the Quincy district of Alexandria, Virginia, a* *gas station owner found two flags — Old Glory and the flag of Virginia — lying on the dusty pavement. An accident? Wind damage? No. Someone had deliberately taken a brick and knocked the cleats off those poles. Now, why am I whining about vandalism when there are murderers and terrorists on the loose? Two words — no respect . . ."*

Aiden frowned. Why did that story sound so familiar?

All at once, he was out of his seat, practically dancing around Agent Ortiz. "We've got to get home! Now!"

Ortiz raised an eyebrow. "What's the big hurry?"

He knew it would sound crazy, but he had to say it anyway: "I think I know where Meg is."

13

In the shadow of the swing set where he and Meg had once played, Aiden confronted the FBI agent who had contributed more than anyone else to the Falconer family's sorrows.

Harris listened patiently as Aiden told him of the incident at the school where Meg had brought down the American flag.

The tall man took a sip of his coffee. "An accident —freak hit with a baseball bat."

"Now the same thing has happened in Alexandria," Aiden persisted. "Two flags, side by side. That can't be a coincidence."

Harris shrugged. "Vandalism. Happens all the time, especially in a district like Quincy that's all factories and warehouses. Nobody lives there. The whole area empties out at night. There's *nothing* to connect that act to Meg."

Aiden was growing frustrated. "You're not listening. Meg got into a lot of trouble over that flag thing. She knows I'd remember. This is a message from her. I'm positive."

The FBI man tried to be kind. "I hear what you're saying. But you have to admit it's pretty flimsy. Ever been to Quincy? It goes on for miles—hundreds of buildings, half of them abandoned. It takes manpower to search an area like that—manpower I don't have and couldn't get if I asked for it. Not on a hunch."

Aiden knew his theory sounded far-fetched. But there was something inside of him—something tied to Meg—that was sure this wasn't just a hunch. "Picture it, Agent Harris. She gets away from her kidnappers for just a few seconds. No one's around; everything's closed; no way to reach a phone. And then she sees these two flagpoles."

Harris hesitated. It was a long shot—the kind of conjecture that could only come from a desperate family member. Yet there was a tiny part of the improbable story that rang true. As fugitives, the Falconer kids had depended on each other 1,000 percent—so much so that they were often thinking with a single mind. If Meg had the chance to send a message, it made perfect sense that she'd send it to her brother. If the kidnappers were near, she couldn't use a signal they'd be able to catch. She'd have to choose something only Aiden would know was a signal. . . .

"Tell you what," he said finally. "I'll call over to Alexandria PD. I'll let them know what's going on, ask them to keep an eye open."

"That's no good!" All of Aiden's frustrations exploded. "That's like saying while you're writing parking tickets, if you happen to notice a kidnapped girl tied up in the backseat, report it! If you won't do this right, I will! My dad and I will go over to Alexandria and search those warehouses ourselves!"

"Your father," Harris reminded him, "has agreed to play things my way, because that's what's best for Meg. I know you think we're all idiots at the FBI. But this is not my first kidnapping. A case like this requires calm professionalism, not going off on a wild-goose chase after a lead that's probably nothing."

Aiden's face twisted with anger. "I don't know why I bothered coming to you! You don't care what happens to my sister! Our family is nothing to you but another promotion!"

Harris watched him turn on his heel and stomp away. The degree to which the Falconer kids hated him always stung a little. Not that he blamed them.

The truth was the more he thought about the conversation with Aiden, the more he felt the boy's theory deserved attention. It was clearly a stretch. And yet—

For two months, those two kids had avoided capture

by the law and murder at the hands of a trained killer. Their survival had depended on unpredictable desperate acts just like the one Aiden was describing. Sending a message by breaking flagpole cleats? Totally crazy. And also totally Falconer.

But if I call Quantico and ask for twenty agents to search the area around a pair of dropped flags, I'll get laughed out of the Bureau. The higher-ups would never go for it.

He downed what was left of his coffee, wincing at the taste of the grainy sludge at the bottom of the cup. Maybe the FBI would refuse to assign any agents to this. But Hank Brajansky was on vacation this week, just hanging around home. Brajansky owed Harris a favor. And he lived on the Virginia side.

Harris reached for his cell phone.

14

HELP ME.

MY NAME IS MARGARET FALCONER, AND I HAVE
BEEN KIDNAPPED BY TWO MEN AND A WOMAN. I'M
BEING HELD IN AN ABANDONED WAREHOUSE. I DON'T
KNOW WHERE, EXCEPT THAT IT'S IN VIRGINIA. IF YOU
ARE READING THIS NOTE, YOU ARE VERY CLOSE. LOOK
FOR AN ELECTRICAL CABLE COMING IN THROUGH A
FIRST-FLOOR WINDOW. THAT'S HOW WE GET POWER
HERE.

MOST OF THE TIME THEY'VE GOT ME LOCKED IN A
WINDOWLESS STOREROOM IN AN OFFICE AREA ON THE
MAIN FLOOR. WHEN I'M IN ANY OTHER PART OF THE
BUILDING, THEY'RE WATCHING ME, USUALLY HOLDING
ON TO ME. THEY DON'T TRUST ME BECAUSE I NEARLY
ESCAPED ONCE.

PLEASE CALL THE POLICE. I'VE SEEN THEIR FACES,
AND I'M AFRAID OF WHAT THAT MIGHT MEAN.

Meg looked up from the piece of paper she'd been
writing on. It was completely blank. The one pen in the

storeroom was bone-dry. Her message was hard-etched on the back of a 1978 brochure for children's hockey equipment. As it was, nobody would ever see it for anything more than an outdated price list for skates and pads. But Meg wasn't finished with it yet.

On a corner shelf piled high with empty binders Meg had found an old glass ashtray, filled to overflowing with cigarette butts and ashes.

Good old 1978, she thought, sifting through the gray-black dust. *The golden age of smoking.* She had spent the last hour working at the stuff with her fingers, grinding it into a powder. It was gross and still smelled bad after all these years, but she prayed it would suit her purpose.

Her fingers were now black with ash, but that was the point. When she was sure that the whole load was as fine as she could make it, she dumped the contents of the tray onto her note and began to smear it back and forth across the paper.

The result was even better than she'd hoped. The ash stained the entire page, leaving the etched lettering standing out, stark white.

Now she had the message. But how on earth was she going to deliver it? The closest she ever came to the outside world was when her captors allowed her to use the bathroom. Even then, the woman went in with her and waited right outside the stall. No one was ever going to let her near a door, or even a window.

The kidnappers no longer wore their rubber masks. What would be the point after she'd already seen their faces? Since she had no other names to go by, Meg still thought of them in terms of their disguises. The large, bearded man was Spidey, the younger man was Mickey, and the woman was Tiger. The Three Animals.

Lucky me.

Spidey had a bad temper and an even worse attitude, backed up by the body of a professional wrestler. He was nasty and menacing. Meg had no trouble believing that he was capable of harming her.

Tiger was much less volatile. But in a way, Meg found her even scarier. She went through the motions of being pleasant, reassuring Meg that they meant her no harm and that everything was going to turn out all right. But her eyes were ice-cold, her manner all business. After Meg's escape attempt, Spidey had ranted and raved and threatened. But it was Tiger who had said matter-of-factly, "Try that once more and you'll never see home again."

Mickey was the only one Meg considered a human being. True, he was a kidnapper, a criminal. But he was kind and always seemed to look embarrassed and regretful whenever he was guarding her.

Meg sensed this and tried to take advantage of it. She started with compliments—how nice he was, how decent, how fair, not like the others. "Why would you risk going to prison for those two? A sweet guy like you wouldn't last five minutes in jail. Believe me, I know. I was in Juvie, and that's nothing compared to adult time. My parents tell stories that would curl your hair!"

Mickey didn't answer, but he didn't get mad, either. He appeared to be thinking it over.

"Listen, it's not too late to get out of this," she pushed on. "If you let me go, I'll tell the cops you were good to me, and that you probably saved my life. Don't risk your whole future—"

"Shut up!" he exploded suddenly. "You know nothing about my future! You know nothing about *me*! You think I'm proud of this? You think I put *kidnapper* when my class wrote essays on 'what I want to be when I grow up'?"

"Then why—?"

He cut her off. "For the *money*, okay? I'm doing this because I need the money, period!"

Meg seized on this. "So this whole thing is for money? You're holding me for ransom?"

Mickey clammed up and refused to speak anymore.

Her mind was in overdrive. Here it was, the answer

to the biggest question of all — the *why*. This had nothing to do with HORUS Global, or her parents' imprisonment. These weren't Falconer haters out for revenge. She had been kidnapped for ransom — a crime for money, pure and simple.

The small measure of relief that came from knowing the truth fizzled in a hurry. Where were Mom and Dad going to get ransom money? They weren't rich people; they were college professors. Besides, their savings had been blown on lawyers back in the days of the trial.

The anguished words were on the tip of her tongue: *We can't pay ransom! My parents are broke*—

She clamped her jaw shut. The kidnappers didn't know that yet. They probably thought the Falconers were rolling in cash. They were famous. There would be book deals, movie deals, wrongful imprisonment lawsuits, and a big settlement from the government.

Maybe. But right now there was nothing.

Meg hesitated. If the kidnappers realized that, would they let her go?

Don't be stupid!

She'd seen their faces. She could describe them to the police. At this point, the promise of ransom might be the only thing keeping her alive.

But that won't last forever. Sooner or later, the kidnappers will figure out that Mom and Dad can't pay. And then what happens?

She touched the pocket of her jeans, where her SOS letter was hidden.

It was more important than ever to find a way to sneak this out of the building.

15

Mornings were the hardest for Aiden, even worse than the worried sleeplessness of nighttime. Morning was when he had to lurch out of an exhausted slumber, only to remember yet again the awful truth of what had happened to his sister. The split second of grogginess before that terrible memory kicked in was the best part of his day.

The routine was always the same. He would get dressed and join his parents in pushing scrambled eggs around a plate. Dad invariably burned the toast, but no one complained. No one had any intention of eating it anyway.

But that morning, as Aiden was pulling on his shirt, he heard a commotion from below. Running a hand through his tousled hair, he rushed downstairs to see the usual FBI crew in a state of high excitement. Mom and Dad were right in the middle of it, scrambling into coats as Agent Harris urged them on from the doorway.

"Let's *go*!"

"Wait for me!" Aiden threw on a jacket and stepped

into sneakers, pulling on the backs as he hopped to keep up. He followed his parents into Harris's Trailblazer. "What's happening? Where are we going?"

"There's been a break in the case," his father told him tensely. "Someone saw Meg."

A Taser could not have brought Aiden to such sudden alertness. "Where? In Alexandria?"

"No," Harris said blandly. "Pikesville."

Aiden was taken aback. Pikesville was in Maryland, just outside Baltimore. It was nowhere near Alexandria, Virginia. He had been so sure that the flagpole incident had been a sign from Meg.

So the FBI had been right not to act on his warning.

"I know I don't have to tell anybody here to stay by the car and not to interfere with the operation," Harris lectured as they drove. "We do our work a whole lot better without civilians getting in the way. Remember, any interference could put Meg in danger."

"We appreciate your letting us come along," said Louise Falconer stiffly. "You can trust us, I promise you."

As Pikesville grew closer, Aiden's belly tightened. After all the time he'd spent praying for this moment to come, it seemed to be happening too fast. They were heading for a confrontation with the kidnappers, with Meg's life hanging in the balance. What if something went wrong? What if there was shooting? What if the kidnappers panicked and —

His nervous thoughts were interrupted when the Trailblazer swung into a cul-de-sac of modest homes and pulled up to a police cruiser that was blocking the street. Harris rolled down the window, and an agent leaned into the SUV. It was Ortiz, Aiden's escort from yesterday.

"Is the team in place?"

"They're waiting for you," Ortiz confirmed. He winked at Aiden. "How's it going, kid?"

Aiden was too scared to do anything but nod.

It did not calm his frazzled nerves to watch Harris swing his long legs out of the SUV and shrug into a king-size bulletproof vest.

"Who called this in?" Harris asked.

"Neighbor," Ortiz replied. "Said she saw a girl matching Margaret's description being carried into number sixty-three just after dawn this morning."

"Okay," said Harris. "Let's do it."

The Falconers stayed with Ortiz at the operation perimeter, scarcely daring to breathe. Aiden stood between his mother and father, the family clinging together for moral support. Their anxiety was almost visible as an aura around them.

Aiden was amazed at the depth of his fear. As a fugitive, he had faced a violent death from point-blank range time and time again. But this—watching from a safe distance—was worse. He had no control over what was going to happen.

There were six agents in the assault team, backed up by two sharpshooters with high-powered rifles. Harris was the leader. In his bulky vest, he had the silhouette of Shaquille O'Neal—an imposing figure as he approached the front door of number 63.

And then the operation was under way—a blur of sound and motion. No warning was given. The door was kicked in, and armed agents swarmed into the house.

"FBI!"

Shouts rang out from inside. Aiden listened intently. It was mayhem, but the noise he feared the most—gunfire—never came.

The agents began to clear the building. A man emerged first, followed by a woman. And then—the Falconers squeezed one another so tightly that Aiden felt genuine pain—

It was a preteen girl with short dark hair. She was the right age, the right height, the right build. But Aiden would have known at any distance that this was not Meg.

A mournful sigh escaped the three Falconers.

It was a false alarm.

16

When Mickey opened the door of Meg's storage closet to ask if she needed a bathroom break, he was startled when a paper airplane sailed past his ear.

"Hey, what are you doing?"

"Trying to keep from dying of boredom," she replied, folding a new plane. "It isn't exactly Disneyland in here."

His eyes scanned the room. "Where did you get that paper?"

"Some old catalog inserts. I think this place used to make sports stuff for kids." He looked suspicious, so she added, "Come on, how can a couple of paper airplanes help me escape? Here—watch this."

With a delicate flick of her wrist, she sent the elaborately folded plane through a series of loops and barrel rolls until it landed gently at his feet.

He bent down to pick it up. "There's no way you could ever do that again."

"Oh, yeah? Give it here." The craft's next flight was almost a perfect duplication of the last.

Mickey's eyes narrowed. "Give me a sheet of that paper." He folded a standard model and launched it with a full windup that would not have been out of place on a pitcher's mound. The plane screamed across the storeroom and flattened its nose against the far wall.

"Not bad," Meg said grudgingly. "But you're building for speed and distance. In a small space, you need more finesse."

Six aircraft later, Mickey still had not mastered finesse. So he went back to his old design, bringing Meg out to the factory floor so their planes could "let it all hang out."

This was exactly what Meg had been hoping for. She kept her eyes peeled for Spidey and Tiger, but there was no sign of the other two kidnappers. She had heard them leaving earlier that morning and had to assume they had not yet returned. Mickey probably wouldn't have released her from her cell if they'd been around.

He ushered her out onto the warehouse floor, deadbolting the entrance to the office area behind them with a key. "No tricks," he warned.

"Gotcha." There was no way out of this section anyway—not unless she could summon the strength to tear open a padlocked steel garage door.

Equipped with four airplanes apiece, Mickey and Meg established themselves on a small low platform that had probably once supported a heavy machine and began testing their skills. They flew for distance and accuracy, swapping secrets of flap folding and nose design, and even laughing a little. It all seemed so comfortable, so *normal*, that Meg could almost forget that her companion was not a friend, but a felon who was holding her for ransom.

But she didn't forget. The true purpose of all this never left her mind for an instant. As they wrangled over speed versus maneuverability, Meg was very much aware of the SOS note in her pocket. It felt larger than a folded piece of paper, as if its importance to her survival had given it added heft. She scanned her surroundings, searching for a crack or hole large enough to slip the letter through.

The factory windows were broken in sections, boarded up in others. Her sharp eyes spotted it — a single pane of glass broken cleanly across one corner, creating a triangular hole just large enough to pass a tennis ball.

But how could she get to it? It had to be fourteen feet off the floor. In Dad's books, Mac Mulvey would have formed the letter into a paper airplane and sailed it right through the hole. That was why Mac Mulvey was fiction, and pretty bad fiction at that. Not even the paper airplane champion of the world — if the title existed — could thread the needle with such a perfect shot.

Drawing her gaze back from the window, she spied

the rolling staircase. The plan emerged full-blown. She made a couple of adjustments to the wing flaps of her plane, reared back, and let fly.

The first attempt missed the staircase, but the second soared high in the air and came to rest on the third step from the top.

"Look at that altitude!" She ran to the wheeled structure and jumped aboard. It looked like the most casual thing in the world. But in reality, it was a carefully calculated move. Her forward momentum started the squeaky casters turning. The apparatus rolled the few feet to the wall and stopped with a jolt.

"Whoa!" Meg exclaimed, making a great show of keeping her balance.

"Hey!" Mickey began. "What are you—?"

But she was already scampering up the stairs to retrieve her plane. As she bent to pick it up, she twisted her back to the window, eased the SOS letter out of her pocket, and dropped it deftly through the hole. Then, cradling her errant aircraft, she danced innocently down the staircase.

She made it about halfway before the door to the office suites was hurled open, and a raging Spidey exploded onto the scene, howling like a madman.

"What's going on? What's she doing out here?!"

Mickey was obviously startled. "Nothing," he whined. "We were just fooling around with paper airplanes."

"Do you think this is *kindergarten*? Are you forgetting what she did two days ago? Can't we trust you with anything? What's so hard about sitting outside a locked room, making sure nobody escapes? What is it about what we're trying to do that you don't understand?"

He said a lot more, and at top volume, before mounting the metal stairs and grabbing Meg by the arm and collar. It hurt—a lot. But Meg didn't make a sound. She refused to give this horrible man the satisfaction of knowing he was getting to her.

He dragged her back into the office area and heaved her bodily into the storeroom.

Tiger appeared in the doorway. "Catch," she said, and tossed something large and flat in Meg's direction.

By reflex, Meg reached up and snatched it out of the air.

"Say cheese." The female kidnapper produced a small digital camera and snapped a picture.

Blinking to clear her eyes after the flash, Meg realized what she held in her hands. It was a copy of *USA Today*. "What—?"

"For your parents," Tiger explained. "So they'll know you're okay."

She said it encouragingly, but the quiet iciness of her voice made the words more terrifying than the most brutal of threats.

She slammed the door and turned the lock. In the background, Spidey could still be heard yelling at Mickey.

Meg dropped the newspaper as if Tiger's touch had imbued the front page with acid. By sheer force of will, she shut out the unpleasantness that surrounded her, replacing it with a single mental picture. It was the SOS letter, dropping from the hole in the window and fluttering to the street below.

She wished it a silent Godspeed.

17

Crushing, devastating disappointment.

There was no other way to describe it. Aiden barely had the strength to hold himself upright as he listened to his mother's sobs and his father's ineffectual attempts to comfort her. The urge to sink down to the ground was almost irresistible.

Gradually, the story came out of the girl they'd thought was Meg. It was very simple, actually. She and her father had driven up from Fort Lauderdale in an all-night marathon. Exhausted, she had fallen asleep and had been carried into the house. A "helpful" neighbor had seen her and noticed that she matched the description of the missing Margaret Falconer. He had called the FBI's tip line.

Agent Harris was grim when he returned to the SUV. "Sorry to put you through this. We really thought we'd caught a break."

"We know it's not your fault," said John Falconer in a thready voice. "You have to follow every lead."

"Not every lead!" Aiden's dashed hopes morphed suddenly into anger. "What about Alexandria?"

"I've got it covered," Harris told him.

Aiden was taken aback. He had been under the impression that Harris was ignoring his flagpole theory. Even Mom and Dad, desperate for hope, had found it far-fetched.

But before Aiden could ask for more information, an ABC news mobile unit pulled up to the house at number 63, and a crew hopped out.

Agent Ortiz groaned. "How did the press get wind of this?" It was the last thing the FBI wanted — national coverage of a false alarm.

Harris shrugged. "How do they ever? Anonymous tips, local police radio, tarot cards. I'll talk to them. Maybe I can convince them to keep a lid on it."

Soon though, it became apparent that no lid would be large enough to contain this story. Within half an hour, news vans from CNN and other networks were on the scene. The newspaper reporters came soon after, along with the wire services. The Falconers were stuck there because Harris's Trailblazer was too boxed-in to move.

The agent himself was embroiled in countless interviews, explaining over and over why the FBI had raided the house of completely innocent people. On Harris's or-

ders, no one was given access to the Falconers. The closest the media got to them was by zoom lens.

The impromptu news conference broke up just before
noon. Most of the reporters had left the street, and Harris was folding his six-foot-seven-inch frame behind the
steering wheel when one final member of the press arrived on the scene, burning rubber in his Toyota Prius.

Aiden recognized the car immediately. "That's the
Blog Hog!"

The tiny vehicle screeched to a halt behind them and
out jumped Rufus Sehorn, his inevitable laptop tucked
under his arm.

Harris gunned the SUV's engine. "You're not talking
to that bottom-feeder." He rolled down the window and
called to Ortiz. "That guy gets no access, you hear me?
Not a comment, not a word, not a grunt."

"What have you got against Rufus?" Aiden complained. "Of all the media, he's the only guy who's trying
to help us."

Harris put the car in gear and stepped on the gas. Sehorn stepped right out in front of the grill, waving the
laptop urgently.

Don't tempt me, little man, the agent muttered to himself. But he braked. "You're too late, pal. I've got nothing
for you."

The Blog Hog was beside himself, his wide hobbit

eyes shining with excitement. "But I've got something for you! It came on my Web site!"

"What is it?" Harris sneered. "Cheap flights to places I don't want to go?"

"No," the blogger told him. "A ransom note."

Doctors J. & L. Falconer—

We have your daughter. These instructions must be followed to the letter if you want her back.

Place two million dollars in unmarked bills in a duffel bag. The money is to be carried by your son, Aiden. Tomorrow afternoon, he will bring it to the phone booth at the corner of Ninth Street and University Avenue in Baltimore. At exactly two P.M., the phone will ring, and he will receive further instructions.

If he is watched by police, there will be CONSEQUENCES. If he is not alone, there will be CONSEQUENCES. If the courier is anyone other than Aiden, there will be CONSEQUENCES.

Do not underestimate us. We do not wish to harm your daughter, but we are deadly serious.

Harris's laptop computer sat on the Falconers' kitchen table, displaying the ransom demand that had been sent to *www.bloghog.usa*. The agent scrolled past the message to reveal a digital photograph. A high-pitched gasp escaped the Doctors Falconer. It was their daughter, Meg, frightened and miserable, in a darkened room, holding up a copy of *USA Today*. She had never seemed younger.

"It's today's paper," Harris confirmed. "We've got no choice but to treat this as genuine."

"Of course it's genuine!" Louise Falconer snapped impatiently. "Look at her—the poor child is scared half to death!"

"Can you trace the e-mail?" her husband put in.

Harris shook his head. "The sender knew what he was doing. According to our tech center, the message was bounced all over the world before it came to the Blog Hog. It could be months before we know the source. By then—" The agent thought better of finishing that sentence and took a sip of coffee. "Obviously, we don't have that kind of time. We've got till tomorrow to make our move, and that calls for a decision from you."

"What decision?" Louise was close to panic. "Where are we going to get two million dollars?"

"The Bureau has access to emergency funds for situations like this," Harris explained.

"To pay ransom demands?" John Falconer was amazed. No criminologist could envision the U.S. government using taxpayer money to reward kidnappers. His eyes narrowed. "You're talking about setting a trap, aren't you? With our daughter's life in danger!"

"No!" his wife exclaimed vehemently. "If the kidnappers find out, they'll kill her!"

"We'll take steps to make sure that doesn't happen," Harris vowed. "We'll get it right. You have my word."

"We spent fourteen months in prison precisely because you got it *wrong*!" John raged. "Your guarantees mean less than nothing in this house! How can we be sure that your surveillance team won't be spotted? Or that the agent you send with the money won't make a mistake?"

"The money won't be with an agent," Harris told them gravely. "The instructions are very clear. *Aiden* has to deliver the ransom, nobody else."

"Absolutely not," snapped Louise. "These people tried to take him when they took Meg. Why would we serve him up on a silver platter?"

"He'll be protected," Harris assured them.

"He *can't* be protected," John insisted. "If your agents have to rescue Aiden, that exposes the trap. And where does that leave Meg?"

The truth was plain on Harris's face. John Falconer's concerns were well founded. The FBI could control this operation only so much. At best, it would be a calculated risk.

Louise was adamant. "I won't gamble one of my children in the hope of saving the other, and chance losing them both."

Another voice spoke, quiet but bedrock steady. "I'm doing it."

The three wheeled to find Aiden standing behind them. His chin was out, his posture ramrod straight, the picture of defiance. "Don't talk about this like we have a choice. We may never get another shot at bringing Meg back alive."

The Falconers regarded their son. He was still the gangly fifteen-year-old they knew. But weeks as a fugitive had added a toughness and courage they had never seen before. Whether or not to deliver the ransom was no longer their choice.

It was his.

Pressure.

Aiden was aware of it as a physical force, crushing down on him, pinning him to his bed.

He couldn't explain it, but somehow he had always known that the quest to bring Meg home would ultimately fall upon him. It felt right, almost comfortable —

Except for the fear.

No amount of time as a fugitive could ever prepare him for that. The stakes were too high — Meg's life.

The mere thought of it made him tremble.

A knock at the door interrupted his uneasy reverie. Aiden sat up to find Agent Ortiz leaning in from the hall.

"Hope I'm not disturbing you. Your buddy's downstairs — the kid with the baseball hat." The FBI man smiled slightly. "Don't worry, nobody tackled him this time."

Richie. Talk about perfect timing. The night before ransom day, and he was here to try again. Aiden should have known he'd be back. Such was the stubbornness of the Greenville Cubs' number-one fan.

Aiden gave the agent an uncomfortable look. "Couldn't you kind of — you know — get rid of him?"

"He's not a bad kid," said Ortiz. "Kind of persistent . . ."

"I'll deal with him eventually," Aiden promised. "Just not now. Okay?"

"Got it."

He listened to the agent's footsteps on the stairs. This time, he felt none of his usual guilt for blowing off Richie. Tomorrow was just too important.

He couldn't cloud his mind with anything else.

"**N**othing personal, kid, but you're going to have to lay off until things quiet down."

Ortiz's words rang in Richie's ears as he trudged across the lawn.

Why doesn't Aiden get it? Of course, I know this is a tough time!

That was the whole point — friends sticking together.

Can't he see that I'm just trying to help?

The sudden voices startled him. Two agents stood smoking cigarettes in front of a pine tree. One of them, he was pretty sure, was the man who had pulled a gun on him during his last visit.

". . . for a family of traitors, these people sure get their fair share from the government. Every time I come back, there are a few more guys assigned to this place."

"Traitors or not," the other agent replied, "that's one tough kid. When I was fifteen, I didn't have the guts to ride the subway by myself, let alone carry two mil into the middle of Baltimore to ransom my kidnapped sister."

"So that's on?" asked the first man.

"Two o'clock," his partner confirmed. "It's going down at the pay phone at Ninth and University. Minimum surveillance—the big man's taking no chances we'll get rumbled. He's treating this like it's his own family."

Richie was astounded. Aiden never talked about his fugitive days. Was this the kind of James Bond stuff that had gone on? Huge money, mysterious meetings, FBI surveillance—it was like something out of a movie!

The kind of ordeal no one should ever have to go through alone.

19

Meg had never been a newspaper person, but she devoured *USA Today* from cover to cover, savoring every word. After being locked up for days, something to read—something to *do*—was almost as welcome as rescue. It could not soothe her fear, but at least it relieved some of the bottomless boredom of life in the storeroom.

She pored over stories from Tulsa and Tokyo, the opinion pages, the TV listings, the crossword puzzle.

You never appreciate a weather forecast until you're stuck in a place where you can't see the sky.

At first, she had just been looking for news about her own case. All she found was a tiny piece on page 7A — NO LEADS IN FALCONER KIDNAPPING. It stated simply that the authorities were still waiting to hear from her captors.

That was confusing. What about the ransom? The kidnappers wanted money. Mickey had admitted it. Why was nothing happening?

She received the answer to that question when Mickey came to take her for a bathroom break. He seemed even jumpier than usual. When she asked him, "What's up?" he carefully avoided her gaze and made no reply.

She pushed open the bathroom door and stepped inside.

"Get her out of here!" shrieked Tiger. *"Now!"*

As Mickey pulled her backward by the collar, Meg caught a glimpse of the female kidnapper. The woman was standing in front of the mirror, painting her face stark white.

What's up with that?

Meg couldn't begin to guess. But one conclusion could be drawn: Something big was about to go down — and soon.

She had to be ready.

The transmitter was small — about the size of a thimble. It disappeared easily under Aiden's sweatshirt, taped to his skin. Harris and the FBI would be able to hear everything Aiden heard. The device would also serve as a panic button — he could sound the alarm if he found himself in danger.

Aiden was more worried about the receiver plugged into his left ear. Yes, it was made of clear plastic, but what if the kidnappers spotted it? The word "consequences" had been haunting him ever since the ransom e-mail.

Harris tried to be reassuring. "I know it seems like you're walking into the lion's den. But this is a controlled situation. My people will be all around you, even though you won't see them."

"I'm not worried about Aiden seeing them," John Falconer said anxiously. "I'm worried about Meg's captors seeing them."

As nerve-racking as this was for Aiden, it was even worse for his parents. Mom and Dad didn't know who to worry about first — their child who was already kidnapped, or the one who was being dangled like a worm on a hook.

Dad drove Aiden into Baltimore in the family car. No Bureau vehicle followed behind it. Harris was determined to give the impression that the kidnappers' instructions were being followed exactly — no FBI; just Aiden alone, taken to the rendezvous by his father.

Aiden had been to Baltimore dozens of times before. Now he looked at the city streets as if observing an alien planet. The feeling of unreality was magnified by the burden he carried in his lap — a duffel containing two million dollars in cash. The bag bore the logo of a local high school athletic department. Harris's idea: "You're a football player bringing your gear home from practice."

"I'm a mathlete," Aiden had told him, and almost smiled. Meg, the athlete in the family, teased him relentlessly about his two left feet.

The bag contained more money than Aiden would

ever see in his life. Yet neither he nor his father cared enough to open the zipper to look at it. Money was nothing. Meg was all that mattered.

The drop-off was even tougher than he'd expected. His father was an emotional wreck. "Someday I hope to be able to make this up to you and your sister. I'm finding it hard to believe what's happened to us—what's *still* happening to us."

"Dad—you can't blame yourself. You have no control over any of this."

"That's right," John Falconer agreed huskily. "I have no control over anything anymore. How can I call myself a father if there's nothing I can do to protect my children?"

"Aiden—" Harris's voice in the earpiece was so close, so clear, that it sounded like it was being beamed straight into Aiden's brain. "Please tell your father that this isn't the time or place."

It was eerie to have the FBI eavesdropping on every word.

"We're cool," he mumbled in reply.

In reality, Aiden was anything but. His body trembled as he got out of the car, and it wasn't just because of the forty-five pounds of hundred-dollar bills in the duffel hanging off his shoulder.

"I'm starting down Ninth Street," he whispered.

"We've got you," Harris told him. "There's a GPS transmitter in the microphone. We're monitoring your position."

The agent was in a high-tech vehicle called the MCC—mobile command center. It looked like an ordinary minivan, but he could direct the entire operation from inside, with a communication link to Aiden as well as the undercover people in the field.

Where were they? Aiden scanned the area. The streets were crowded, but he couldn't tell which of the many pedestrians were Harris's operatives.

That's what undercover means, he reminded himself. *Nobody's supposed to know who you are.*

He could see the pay phone now, two blocks ahead. His watch read three minutes to two.

It's happening . . . it's really happening. . . .

Hurrying to beat the light, he stepped onto the corner of Ninth Street and University Avenue. Suddenly, standing in front of the pay phone, Aiden Falconer was hit with an almost overwhelming sense that he was being watched.

Of course you're being watched, he chided himself. *Half the FBI's out here with you!*

But real undercover agents were trained to be invisible. This was something different. Could it be the kidnappers, coming for their money?

Maybe there would be no call with instructions. The drop would happen right here, right now! Meg's captors might be just a few steps away. . . .

The phone rang.

20

FBI Agent Hank Brajansky cursed the day he'd ever met Emmanuel Harris.

This was the second precious vacation day he'd wasted pounding the cracked pavement of the Quincy district of Alexandria—a grimy neighborhood of ancient factories and warehouses. For reasons he refused to explain, Harris suspected that the kidnapped Falconer girl might be in one of these crumbling structures.

"I never should have borrowed the big man's coffeepot," Brajansky complained to his companion, Ernie Hoag.

Hoag laughed. "Borrowing it wasn't the problem. You never should have busted it."

"How was I supposed to know it was some kind of imported French press thingamabob?" Brajansky surveyed the cityscape helplessly. "Hundreds of buildings, half of them abandoned. I'm supposed to be home, for Pete's sake."

"What would you be doing at home?" Hoag challenged. He had just retired from the FBI last year. He was so bored with golf that he was overjoyed to help with any kind of police work. "Lying on the couch in front of the Weather Channel?"

"Two more weeks of hurricane season. It beats slogging through garbage and old newspapers—" Brajansky froze. In the windblown litter at his feet, a single white page stood out from the others. The writing was white against a dark gray background.

Brajansky bent down to pick it up. The words leaped at him:

> **HELP ME.**
> **MY NAME IS MARGARET FALCONER, AND I HAVE**
> **BEEN KIDNAPPED . . .**

"What does it say?" asked Hoag eagerly.

"It says Harris isn't as crazy as he looks!" Brajansky exclaimed. "Come on, we've got to find this kid!"

Breathlessly, Aiden answered the ringing pay phone.

"Hello?"

"Cross the street and keep on walking," ordered a gruff voice. "There's an open garbage can with a red shoe-box on top."

"Where's my sis—?"

Click. The line went dead.

"Did you hear?" Aiden breathed to Harris over the wire. "He said I should—"

"We got it," Harris acknowledged. "Follow instructions unless I tell you different."

I'm playing the kidnappers' game, Aiden thought, stepping into the road. *A game I can't control.*

Who knew what trap might lie ahead? His eyes darted from face to face, scanning passersby, trying to identify FBI agents.

What if Harris is lying? What if I'm all alone?

Yet the feeling that he was being watched was even stronger than before.

He had never felt so exposed.

There it was! He could see the red shoe-box, sitting on top of a green lawn bag in an overstuffed steel can. With trembling hands, he picked it up.

Empty?

No, not empty. Something was rattling around in there.

"What is it, Aiden?" Harris asked in his ear. "What's in the box?"

His heart a pile driver, Aiden lifted the lid. "A pager," he whispered.

"Turn it on," the agent instructed.

Aiden flicked the switch. A high-pitched beeping exploded out of the device. Aiden was so startled that he nearly fumbled it down a sewer grating. But he held on, watching the tiny screen as the message came in.

I SEE YOUR FACE . . .

He looked up suddenly, half expecting to find one of Meg's kidnappers standing right in front of him. But the scene had not changed.

More words marched across the small display.

Harris: "What does it say?"

NO TALKING OR SHE DIES . . .

The reply was partway out of Aiden's mouth when those chilling words hit home. He clenched his jaw and bit down hard. Of course, he had no way of knowing he was really under surveillance.

But how can I take that risk?

"Aiden?" the agent prompted.

Lips sealed, he brought his mouth down to his chest and grunted, "Uh-uh."

"What's that? Say again?"

But Aiden was already reading the rest of the kidnappers' instructions: GO EAST ON NINTH TO FREDERICK DOUGLASS BLVD. YOU HAVE FOUR MINUTES . . .

Aiden flew. The strap of the duffel cut into his shoulder as the weight of the bag turned every step into an agonizing squat-thrust.

Harris was yelling in his ear now, demanding to know what was happening. But all Aiden could think was:

Baltimore's a big place. Frederick Douglass Boulevard could be far! What if I don't make it in time? What'll they do to Meg?

He could see a major intersection coming up. He scanned for a street sign. Thornbury. He blasted across the road, earning himself a chorus of squealing tires, honking horns, and angry shouts. He barely noticed the clamor.

Four minutes! That's so short! Who knows how much time I've got left?

For extra speed, he snatched up the forty-five-pound bag and hugged it to his chest. It doubled as a battering ram to scatter a group of teenage girls blocking the far corner.

In the earpiece, he vaguely noted Harris alerting his people in the field: "Can anybody see the kid? I think he's running . . . no, don't get too close! The operation's still on. . . ."

Another intersection. *Please be Douglass! Please be Douglass . . .*

Douglass! His relief almost knocked him over as he sprinted to the corner. He'd made it—but was he in time?

His answer came in the form of the electronic screech of the pager.

GET ON THE NUMBER 11 BUS HEADING SOUTH . . .

"Bus?" he exclaimed, and almost bit his tongue off. *Keep your mouth shut!* he ordered himself. *Remember what you're doing here!*

He was so flustered that he almost missed it—a line of passengers boarding a Baltimore city bus. He dashed for it, arriving just as the doors began to close with a hydraulic hiss. Out of sheer desperation, he thrust the duffel into the opening. The folding doors stopped dead, pressed against two million dollars.

The driver looked at him in disgust. "Yeah, okay. Get on."

Aiden stared in dismay at the coin box. He was carrying more money than he'd ever dreamed of, but did he have a dollar sixty for the fare? He dug in both pockets, coming up with quarters, dimes, nickels, and pennies.

Half a block behind, a yellow taxi darted into traffic. Its lone passenger leaned anxiously forward, eyes on the back of the bus.

21

Emmanuel Harris's ever-present cup of coffee had spilled all over the floor and was soaking into the carpet of the FBI's Mobile Command Center.

"Help me out, people!" he barked into the microphone. "Tell me somebody's still got a fix on my kid!"

There was a chorus of "Negative" and "Lost him," until Agent Ortiz finally spoke up, his voice a series of gasps, the pounding sound his running footsteps. "He's on a bus, heading south on Douglass! They're pulling away from me!"

"Get a car over there!" Harris bawled.

"We can have a chopper in the air in two minutes," came the voice of the controller from Central Dispatch.

"No!" Harris said sharply. "I don't want to spook the kidnappers. I think they already suspect the kid's wired. That's why he's clammed up."

"We've got two million bucks on the line," the controller reminded him.

"We've got two children on the line," Harris amended. "Nobody does anything until I give the word."

"Hank — look at this!"

Ernie Hoag's voice was subdued, but there was no mistaking his excitement.

Brajansky peered around the corner of the old brick warehouse. Instantly, he spotted what the retired agent had seen. A wire had been strung from the transformer box on the street through a first floor window — exactly what the kidnapped girl's note had described.

This was the place.

"I'll call Harris for backup," Brajansky decided.

Hoag elbowed him hard. "What are you talking about? *I'm* your backup. We don't leave that girl in there for one minute longer than she has to be!"

Against his better judgment, Brajansky agreed. The two followed along the side of the building until they came to a steel door. Brajansky tried the knob. It wouldn't budge. From his pocket, he produced a lock pick and carefully selected the right size tool.

It was the work of perhaps ten seconds. Weapons in hand, they entered the warehouse. Soundlessly, the two surveyed their surroundings by the filtered light coming in the dirty windows. The place was long abandoned, but this seemed to have been some kind of packaging center. Dusty cartons and corrugated boxes were piled around the remains of a conveyor belt.

"Heck of a big place," Hoag whispered. "Let's split up."

Brajansky nodded. With silent hand gestures, the two divided up the building. Hoag headed through the arch to the main manufacturing floor. Brajansky's eyes fell on a back hall clogged with stacked chairs. The note came back to him: . . . *a windowless storeroom in an office area* . . .

Chairs, he thought. *Offices?*

There was only one way to find out.

Aiden struggled into the seat with his two-million-dollar burden.

He was pretty sure he was on his own now. No way had the FBI managed to tail him onto the bus. In his earpiece, he could hear Harris haranguing his agents, exhorting them to stay in range. That meant they were *out* of range, didn't it? They hadn't lost him — they could track his position by GPS —

But a GPS transmitter won't stop bullets if the kidnappers decide they want me out of the way.

Meg's captors had played this perfectly. They obviously knew what they were doing. It was not an encouraging thought.

Did he dare sneak a word to Harris? Surely the kidnappers couldn't see him now. No, it was still too risky.

The vehicle was crowded to the point of discomfort. There could be a spy on board — although it seemed as if most of his fellow passengers were children, and young children at that.

He'd been riding for about ten minutes when the pager came to life again.

GET OFF WHERE THE KIDS GET OFF. FOLLOW THEM. . . .

The words chilled him to the bone. How could the kidnappers know about all the children? Or what stop they'd be going to?

Yet, at the corner of Douglass and Delancey, every single kid on the bus, accompanied by a throng of parents, rose and lined up at the exit. It was astonishing . . . and very scary.

Hefting his duffel, Aiden got off with the others. En masse, the parents and children crossed the street and oozed down the next block. It was obvious they had a destination in mind. But what? And what could it possibly have to do with Meg?

In the distance, he could hear music and, yes, drums.

As Aiden surged along with the crowd, the yellow cab pulled up to the corner of Douglass and Delancey. The lone passenger got out.

He followed at a distance, ducking into doorways and alleys.

His gaze never left the back of Aiden Falconer's head.

For Meg, it was an omen. When the fluorescent fixture in her storeroom prison sizzled and began a dim flickering, the diminished light matched her diminished hopes.

What an idiot she'd been to think anyone would find her letter. Thirty seconds of rain would have reduced it to gray-stained pulp. The wind could have put it two counties away — or up a fifty-foot tree.

No one was coming for her. No one but the kidnappers themselves, the Three Animals. Their plans for her were uncertain.

But I've seen their faces.

Even if, by some miracle, ransom was paid with money the Falconers didn't have, how could they let her go?

Ever since she'd been chased out of the bathroom by Tiger and her white makeup, Meg had known that something was about to happen. Now she knew another thing, too. Whatever was coming, she'd have to face it alone.

The next time that door opened, she could not meekly obey her captors' orders. The time had come to fight for her life.

Her hands tightened on her weapon of choice — the heavy glass ashtray she'd used to mix the "ink" for her ill-fated SOS note. Not exactly firepower, but it was heavy and hard and portable.

There she sat in the flickering gloom, nerves at the breaking point. Yet when the doorknob began to jiggle, she was taken completely by surprise, lulled by the silence outside her cell. She had not heard her captors for close to an hour.

Now one of them was coming for her.

Moving like a cat, she sprang silently up onto a metal shelving unit. The knob slowly turned. Meg tensed, ready to pounce.

There was a click, and the door swung wide, spilling a shaft of outside light across the floor. She timed her leap just as her quarry stepped into the storeroom. With all her might, she slammed her ashtray down on the crown of his head. The glass shattered, tinkling to the floor around the crumpled body of —

Who — ?

22

Meg bent low over the unconscious man, who was middle-aged, with gray hair and a bald spot in the back. He was not one of her three kidnappers.

Oh, God, who did I hit?

She snaked her arm around his inert form and pulled an ID wallet from his breast pocket. She flipped it open.

It was an FBI badge.

They had found her! She was rescued! At least, she *had* been before she'd brained the cavalry.

"Please, mister, wake up! Please—" She checked the ID. "Agent Brajansky?"

Brajansky groaned but did not come to.

Meg whimpered, crushed by the sheer irony of this. Days in captivity— finally, a chance to fight back—

And I conked the wrong guy.

She wrestled the regret out of her mind. A decision had to be made. As badly as she felt about leaving Brajansky here injured, she could not waste this opportunity to escape. Then, once she was out and away, she could send help.

She stepped across the prone agent and dashed down the hall. There was a door around here somewhere, she was sure. But Meg didn't intend to waste time searching for it. She was heading for her escape window. Next stop: freedom.

She turned the corner and spied the office straight ahead. The desk was still under the window, but a piece of plywood had been nailed across the opening. She leaped up onto the blotter, wrapped her fingers around the board, and pulled. The nails grated and released a little but did not come free. She tried again, yanking until her palms were full of splinters. But she could not move the plywood more than an inch from the molding.

In frenzied haste, she snatched up a metal floor lamp and bashed the glass shade off the top. Then she jammed the pole behind the board and put her whole weight into prying the wood from the frame.

With a crunch, the obstruction came away, revealing the opening to the street. Leaving blood smears from her torn palms, she scrambled over the sash and dropped to the sidewalk.

I did it! I'm out!

The thought had barely crossed her mind when a black Buick sedan wheeled around the corner and parked at the curb.

Meg stared in shock and horror. Spidey was at the wheel. His passenger was Mickey.

The moment was a lightning strike. Meg had not expected them, and they were astonished to see her.

With a gasp, she spun around and fled.

Mickey reached for his door handle to give chase, but Spidey ordered, "No!" He drove the big car right up onto the sidewalk, closing the gap with Meg in seconds, dogging her heels.

Meg heard the roar of the engine and felt its heat radiating toward her.

They're going to run me over!

"Stop!" shouted Mickey. "You'll kill her!"

The car's front bumper made contact. Meg squeezed her eyes shut, awaiting an excruciating end. But the delicate collision felt more like a bump across the backside with a shopping cart. It knocked her off her feet, and she tumbled forward. Spidey slammed on the brakes, and the two men were out of the car.

By the time Meg struggled upright, her kidnappers were upon her.

Retired FBI agent Ernie Hoag had just found the office area when the screaming started. He rushed down the hall, coming to a sudden halt at the open door of a large storage closet. There lay his friend Brajansky, bleeding from a head wound, broken glass all around him.

He dropped to his knees and found a pulse. "Hank — can you hear me? Where's the girl?"

When there was no reply, he leaped back up and continued his search for the source of the cries. This place was like a maze, with offices all over. Who knew where the sound could be coming from? One thing, though, was plain: It was a young kid, obviously in trouble. It could only be Margaret Falconer.

Then he saw it. Just outside a scratched and filthy window, two men were manhandling a struggling, protesting girl. The larger of them lifted her bodily, tossed her into the trunk of a dark sedan, and slammed the lid shut.

Hoag may have been retired, but the instincts were automatic. With a dexterity he didn't think he still had, he was across the room, working at the window. It was either locked or jammed. Outside, the two men were getting into the car. Hoag picked up a chair and smashed the glass. He scrambled out to the sidewalk just in time to see the sedan disappearing around the corner.

He reached for his cell phone.

As Aiden approached the end of the block, the crowd grew denser, and he had to hug the duffel tightly to his chest. Using it as a bumper, he pushed through the crush and peered down the next street.

The sight that met his eyes was so bizarre that he wondered if the stress of Meg's abduction had caused him to hallucinate. Two huge gray elephants were walking toward him with a majestic gait that took his breath away.

He put it all together in a flash—elephants, music, sequin-clad trainers, hundreds of kids. A circus parade!

There were tumblers, performers on unicycles, stilt walkers, pipe organs, and animal cages on wheels. It was pure spectacle—

But why would the kidnappers deliberately direct me here?

He looked to his beeper, as if expecting to see the answer scrolling across the screen. The device was silent and dark.

He did a bewildered three-sixty, scanning for some sort of clue—what came next?

That was when his gaze fixed on a figure in a doorway—and an all-too-familiar baseball cap bearing the logo of the Greenville Cubs.

In a city swarming with FBI agents, the guy following me turns out to be Richie?

Aiden was aghast. How had Richie gotten wind of all this? No. Dumb question. He was *here*—in the middle of an operation that could very easily get Meg killed; one that might be falling apart at this moment!

I've got to get rid of him!

But how? Aiden had been forbidden to talk.

Hefting the duffel, he sidled through the still-gathering crowd until he was standing in front of his school friend.

Caught out, Richie tried to explain his presence. "I've got your back, man."

Aiden spun him around and pushed him face-first up against the wall. Then he pressed his own nose to the bricks and hissed, "Get out of here!"

"You need me."

"You're killing my sister!" Aiden seethed.

Richie was completely cowed. "How — ?"

"Go home!"

As Aiden spun around and plowed back into the crowd, a cheer went up among the spectators. The parade route was now multicolored with clowns on Rollerblades. They swarmed everywhere, handing out candy and free circus passes to the kids along the road.

The scene was so chaotic that Aiden almost ignored the commotion in his earpiece — Harris, in a state of high excitement: ". . . dark sedan; two men, one heavyset with a beard, one slight! Last seen at Three-forty-five

Industry in Alexandria — the Quincy district! No shoot-ing — they've got the girl in the trunk!"

Aiden could keep silent no longer. "Is it Meg? You found her?"

"Aiden!" Harris exclaimed. "Are you all right?"

"Where's my sister?"

"She's been spotted, but we don't have her," Harris re-plied. "The operation's off. Stay put. Someone's coming for you."

Aiden was stunned. The plan in tatters, Meg in the trunk of a car. Oh, God —

A clown with a white face and cherry-red nose glided up and held out a lollipop — a woman, he thought, judg-ing by the small features and fine lips. Automatically, Aiden reached out and took the candy. Before he real-ized what was happening, the duffel was snatched from his arms, and the clown sped away with it.

Horrified understanding exploded inside Aiden with the violence of a volcanic eruption. He had just been face-to-face with one of Meg's kidnappers! He remembered the female voice behind the Tiger Woods mask on the day his sister had been taken.

She knows where Meg is! And I let her go!

23

Wild with urgency, he ran out into the middle of the street. The sight that greeted him made his heart sink into his sneakers. There must have been fifty clowns over the length of the parade—a sea of white faces and red noses, all in full flight on their Rollerblades. Finding the right one—

A hand closed on Aiden's shoulder. He turned to see a circus security guard, who told him, "Back to the sidewalk, son."

"Your clown stole my duffel bag!" Aiden blurted.

The man was humorless and impatient. He took a rough grip on Aiden and began frog-marching him over to the curb.

There was the sound of scrambling feet. Suddenly, Richie was clamped onto the man, arms around his neck, legs hugging his midsection, piggyback-style.

"Aiden—*go!*"

Aiden shook himself free and took off after the Rollerblading clowns. "Agent Harris!" he bellowed as he ran. "One of the kidnappers is here! She's in a clown suit! And she's got the money!"

"A *clown suit*?" Harris repeated.

"There are clowns all over the place! It's a circus parade!"

Harris thought it over for a second. "Can you stop the parade?"

"How? I'm not the grand marshal!"

"Find a way," Harris ordered. "Now!"

Aiden looked around helplessly. The only circus official he could see was the security guard who was hustling Richie to the sidewalk. No way would that guy ever help. They wouldn't stop the parade unless something really big happened—like an accident or a medical emergency, or if one of the animals got out of its pen—

No sooner had the thought crossed his mind than a large cage rolled up on a flatbed truck. The high-pitched chattering was unmistakable. Monkeys, screeching and gibbering, at least a dozen of them.

Without thinking, Aiden heaved himself up onto the flatbed, sidled around to the door of the enclosure, and released the snap lock. When the door swung wide, the monkeys, chattering their approval, streamed out at light speed, scattering over the parade and its spectators.

The reaction was bedlam. Onlookers screamed and ran in all directions. The monkeys tested their newfound freedom by using heads as perches and springboards. The jugglers and performers abandoned their routines and began chasing the escaped animals. Some of the clowns joined the hunt. Whistles blew everywhere, and the parade ground to a halt.

Mission accomplished, Aiden jumped down from the truck and pounded through the chaos in search of the kidnapper clown.

Richie appeared at his side. "Where are we going?" he puffed.

At this point, Aiden was grateful for any help he could get. "We're looking for the clown who's got my duffel! But be careful — she's one of the kidnappers!"

They barreled amid milling spectators and circus people, scrutinizing clown after clown. The only one holding anything was wrestling a captured monkey. It was scratching his red nose and white face, shrilling its protest to the world.

"She's gone!" Aiden cried in despair.

Richie pointed. "Look!"

At the other end of the block, the figure of a clown was trying to push past a cluster of terrified spectators in order to reach a side street. The dark shoulder strap of the duffel bag was clearly visible against the fabric of the clown suit.

Aiden and Richie raced over, sidestepping children and airborne monkeys.

Spying Aiden approaching on the run, the kidnapper tried to bull her way through the crowd. But the Rollerblades on her feet were a disadvantage because they gave her no traction.

Aiden busted into the throng, pushing protesting people aside. He reached for her but succeeded only in grabbing the handle of the duffel.

"What have you done with my sister?" he bellowed.

She pulled harder on the bag, but Aiden firmed up his grip. Richie reached in, adding his strength to the tug-of-war. All at once, the strap broke. Richie and the bag flew backward, sprawling on the pavement.

But Aiden wasn't interested in two million dollars. He lunged at the kidnapper clown, determined to capture her and rescue Meg.

And suddenly he was staring down the barrel of a snub-nosed pistol.

There were screams from the onlookers and a stampede to get away. The space around them opened up as if by magic.

"Give me the bag," ordered a cold voice.

Richie scrambled to his feet and moved forward to hand over the duffel.

"Stay back, Rich," Aiden commanded, stepping in front of his friend. "She gets nothing until Meg goes free."

The gun stayed leveled at Aiden's chest. "You're not in a position to bargain."

Richie's voice shook with terror. If he had underestimated the dangers of "helping" Aiden, he did so no longer. "Give it to her, man! She'll shoot you!"

"Let her," Aiden replied evenly, never taking his eyes from the kidnapper. It was not just bravado. He had already decided that he would rather get shot than give up his only link to his sister.

Aiden saw the gun hand twitch and understood how close to death he really was. Fear swelled in his chest, but he did not back down.

The standoff was broken by a squeal from above. In a reddish-brown blur, a small monkey dropped from a lamppost and wrapped itself around the white-painted face.

Aiden leaped forward and went for the gun. The kidnapper held on, even as she swatted at the animal that was blinding her.

Richie jumped to his aid, but Aiden ordered him away. "Go find help!"

His friend stumbled off, dragging the bag beside him. He got about thirty feet before colliding with the burly form of a Baltimore city policeman. The officer took one look at the duffel—the zipper had come undone a few inches, revealing Benjamin Franklin on the face of a neat bundle of hundred-dollar bills. Richie was in handcuffs before he could even begin to explain himself.

With another screech, the monkey leaped onto a mailbox and perched there, scolding the combatants loudly. The kidnapper kicked at Aiden's leg with a rock-hard Rollerblade boot.

"Ow!" Aiden doubled over in pain, and she slammed the gun butt down on the top of his head. A firestorm went off between his ears. He dropped to the street, out cold.

The kidnapper Meg called Tiger stared at the precious duffel, some thirty feet away, and in the hands of a uniformed cop. In the distance, sirens — lots of them — were growing louder.

The odds were no longer in her favor.

She slipped the pistol back into a hidden pocket and glided off to join a group of clowns as they helped round up the loose monkeys. Then she was just one of many, a needle in a haystack.

She was disappointed in today's result, but not angry. They still had their hostage. That was the important thing.

Soon it would be time to disappear from here. A moment of distraction, a quick dash down an alley, clown suit and Rollerblades tossed in the Dumpster, a few moist towelettes to clean off the makeup.

Finally, a young woman in jeans and a sweater would emerge from the lane. Just another passerby, wondering what had happened to disrupt such a pleasant circus parade.

24

Aiden's head wound was treated in Emergency, but he was released immediately.

"You're lucky," Agent Ortiz told him on the ride home. "You should see Brajansky. Concussion."

Aiden sucked air between his teeth. "They're vicious, these kidnappers."

"Actually, we think it was your sister who hit him. Mistaken identity."

Aiden held his aching head. "She could have been *rescued*!"

Yet with everything that had gone wrong today, he was still able to take a tiny amount of comfort in this horrible mishap that had landed Agent Brajansky in the hospital and left Meg in the hands of her captors. What she had done proved she was tough.

She'll need to be to come through this alive.

The reporters were back on his front lawn. They barked questions and photographed his bandaged head as Ortiz delivered him into the arms of his frantic parents.

As awful as the ransom operation had turned out to be, his parents' grief was even harder for him to take.

"I'm fine, Mom," Aiden tried to reassure her. "Don't worry about me. Worry about—" He could not bring himself to finish the sentence.

Meg. The absent Falconer cast a larger shadow than any of them at this moment. Their attempt to get her back had failed, and she was gone.

But that was too terrible to talk about. So Mom and Dad obsessed over Aiden's head, Brajansky's concussion, and the fact that Richie had spent three hours in jail while the FBI and the Baltimore PD had wrangled over custody of the two million dollars.

"Richie really came through for me today," Aiden admitted grudgingly. "He's a good friend." It was a tribute to the legendary Pembleton stubbornness. The kid had been determined to help, and—against all odds—he had.

"Richie needs to keep out of this," put in Agent Harris, entering from the kitchen. "He could have gotten shot today."

"*I* might have gotten shot if he hadn't been there to help me," said Aiden stiffly. "And you've got him to thank for saving your ransom money. Remember, he stayed on my tail when all your trained agents got left in the dust."

Harris had the grace to look embarrassed. "Believe me,

I've been hearing that all day from my bosses and every reporter in town. Your friend the Blog Hog has already started telling the world what incompetents we are."

Louise Falconer was not sympathetic. "Rufus Sehorn's Web site has been our only communication with the kidnappers. We should be giving him whatever information he needs and trusting him to use it well. Maybe they'll contact him again."

"Your trust should be in police work, not Internet gossip," Harris warned. "We've got agents going over every inch of that warehouse. Trace evidence is checking the clown suit we found in the Dumpster. And Hoag has a description of the car and two letters of the license plate. The alert is back up again. We'll find her. It's only a matter of time."

Time. The word hung in the air. How much time did Meg have left?

The sound of grinding metal on metal pulled Meg back from the edge of consciousness. She opened her eyes into the same blackness that had surrounded her for who knew how many hours. She was still in the trunk.

Suddenly, a silver drill bit penetrated the shell around her, punching down toward her face. She screamed and tried to shrink out of its way, conking her head on a tire iron. Hot metal fragments rained down on her cheek.

Horror and disbelief blazed in her heart. *Am I being murdered?*

It seemed like a strangely cruel way to execute a hostage.

All at once, the roar ceased, and the spiraling drill bit pulled back. It was replaced by a tiny shaft of light.

"Think that's enough air?" asked a rough voice. Spidey.

"Another one," Tiger replied.

The roar swelled again, and the drill burst through in another spot.

Air holes. So she wasn't being killed.

Not yet.

She lay there, curled into a shaking ball, banishing the tension from her body as she conquered her terror. The thought that she was still alive was a welcome one. But it took some getting used to.

Earlier, she had thought that the method of her execution would be carbon monoxide. The air in the trunk had been suffocating, the smell of car exhaust overpowering. They had driven around for what had seemed like forever. All Meg had wanted to do was breathe.

She must have been still conscious when they had rendezvoused with Tiger, because she remembered the conversation:

Spidey: "Where's the money?"

And Tiger's furious reply: "That Aiden Falconer will pay for what I suffered today!"

Meg had almost cheered. *Way to go, Aiden!* But that had been the fumes talking. Her one faint chance — that the ransom had been paid, and she was about to be released — was gone. No happy ending. No hope.

When she had finally slipped into a dozing stupor, it had crossed her mind that she would probably never wake up. She had even said a silent good-bye to Mom, Dad, and Aiden. It had just been a moment, and a half-conscious one at that. But it was one she would never, ever forget.

Now, gulping fresh air through newly drilled holes, her backbone stiffened as her head cleared. She *would* see her family again. She couldn't imagine how, but it was going to happen. If the kidnappers thought they had defeated Meg Falconer, they had another thing coming. This black car would not be her coffin!

She had no way of knowing that the black Buick sedan was now pale green. She had no way of knowing that it stood drying in the middle of a huge deserted hangar, west of Washington, D.C., that had once housed a Goodyear blimp.

She had no way of knowing that the search for her was far, far away.

TIME IS RUNNING OUT!

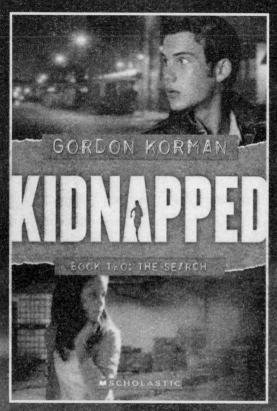

AIDEN DESPERATELY SEARCHES FOR CLUES THAT ONLY HE CAN RECOGNIZE TO FIND HIS SISTER. MEANWHILE, MEG PLANS AN ESCAPE. THE TWISTS AND TURNS COME FAST AND FURIOUS IN THE NEWEST GORDON KORMAN THRILLER.

■SCHOLASTIC

www.scholastic.com

KNPD2T